Also by Dorothy Edwards

Rhapsody

WINTER SONATA

by

DOROTHY EDWARDS

With an introduction by
Dr Claire Flay

HONNO CLASSICS

Published by Honno
'Ailsa Craig', Heol y Cawl, Dinas Powys,
South Glamorgan, Wales, CF64 4AH

1 2 3 4 5 6 7 8 9 10

First published in Great Britain by Wishart & Co, London in 1928
First published by Honno in 2011
This edition ©Honno 2011

© Introduction, Dr Claire Flay 2011

British Library Cataloguing in Publication Data
A catalogue record for this book is available from the British Library.

ISBN 13: 978-1-906784-29-4

Published with the financial support of the Welsh Books Council.

Cover Illustration © Getty Images
Cover design: Graham Preston
Text Design: Elaine Sharples

Printed & bound in Wales by Gomer Press, Llandysul, Ceredigion

Introduction

CLAIRE FLAY

Dorothy Edwards committed suicide on a Cardiff railway line in 1934, at the age of thirty-one, just nine years after the publication of her first short story. Hence her authorial career was by default very short, but during its brief span she produced a small but fascinating body of work.

Biography

Readers of Edwards' 1927 short story collection *Rhapsody* and 1928 novel *Winter Sonata* are often surprised to learn of her background: she gives no explicit indication of her unusual upbringing, her nationality or even her gender in her published work. Distinctly lacking the gritty realist narrative that characterises the work of the Welsh valleys male writers of the early twentieth century, her readers could be forgiven for initially believing hers to be the work of a middle-class English author given the setting and tone of her fiction.

Edwards was, however, raised against the same industrial backdrop that so strongly influenced her male counterparts. The first and only child of Edward and Vida Edwards, Dorothy was born on 18th August 1903 in Ogmore Vale, a small mining community in south Wales. Her father was headmaster of the local school; he was also a vegetarian, an ardent socialist and an active member of the Labour movement, who raised his daughter to believe that a revolution was imminent and that social and sexual divisions would crumble during her lifetime. As a child Edwards often listened to her father and his acquaintances discuss the political issues of the day; key radical socialist politicians, including Independent Labour Party leaders Keir Hardie and Bruce Glacier, were regular visitors to the family home in Ogmore Vale. As an adult, one of her fondest recollections was that of welcoming Hardie onto the stage in Tonypandy during the 1912 miners' strike when she was nine years old, dressed from head to toe in red.

Dazzled by the light of her father's radicalism, Edwards saw her mother by comparison as conventional and staid. "[S]he had to accept the discordant note of my father's red tie, of which indeed I think she came to understand the vital necessity," Edwards recalled in her 1933 diary.[i] Edward Edwards had earned a reputation as a controversial, albeit progressive, figure; the burden of his eccentricities, however, fell wholly on his wife's shoulders. While her husband gave talks about the future of socialism on street corners, or carried out anthropological experiments on the mountainside, Vida "remained in the valley below, and made tea for the committees", expending "much anxiety and pain upon the difficult task of reconciling her husband's revolutionary views with the obvious respectability and merit of the wondering friends and relations, who disagreed with him so emphatically".[ii]

Edward Edwards died in 1917, when his daughter was a fourteen-year-old scholarship boarder at the prestigious Howell's School for Girls, Cardiff. His epitaph indicates the esteem in which he was held by his community: donated by the local branches of the Labour Party, the Trade Unions and the Co-operative Society, it reads "In memory of Edward Edwards, Schoolmaster and Socialist Pioneer." The death of her beloved father at such a formative age had a devastating effect on Edwards, as her subsequent fascination in her work with broken families or missing parents shows. But there were practical implications, too: barely a month after his death, and eighteen years after leaving her teaching career on her marriage, Vida took up a teaching post in the boys' school that her late husband had established two years before. Here she remained for eighteen months until, in March 1919, she was transferred to Ely School in Cardiff, and the family left Ogmore Vale for Rhiwbina.[iii]

Life in Cardiff seemed to suit Edwards. In 1920 she became an undergraduate student of Greek and philosophy at the then University College of South Wales and Monmouthshire (now Cardiff University), where she was popular and active in various societies as well as being a regular contributor to the college magazine, *Cap and Gown*. An engagement to young philosophy lecturer John Thorburn was brief and painful, and provided much fodder for conversation with her close friends, S. Beryl Jones and Winifred Kelly. Edwards graduated in 1924, and shortly afterwards three of her short stories were published in Edgell Rickword's influential but short-lived periodical, *The Calendar of Modern Letters*. A modernist with an eye for talent, Rickword was quick to sign Edwards up for a collection of short stories. Edwards had originally intended to taken singing lessons in Milan after graduating (she had an excellent, semi-trained operatic voice), but a trip to Europe with her mother in 1926 was instead spent finishing the stories included in *Rhapsody*, which appeared in 1927 when she was just twenty-four years old. *Winter Sonata*, conceived during the same trip and finished while visiting Beryl Jones in Yorkshire, was published the following year. Both books received excellent reviews from the London literati. But, after this promising start, Edwards floundered. Feeling trapped in Cardiff, the sole carer for her by now aged and increasingly ill mother, her life became dominated by domestic struggle and depression. In a letter to university friends Jones and Kelly, written during this period, she said: "I can feel another attack of depression coming on. If it is worse than the last, heaven help me."[iv] To another college friend, Sona Rosa Burstein, she wrote, "It is quite impossible for me to believe that I shall ever write anything again."[v] Her remaining fiction publications were all posthumous.

The novel

When Arnold Nettle arrives in a typical English country village on the last day of summer, his greatest hope is that he will make it through the winter months without illness. On his first day as a telegraph clerk in the village post office, Nettle meets, and fancies himself in love with, Olivia Neran. The elder of the two Neran sisters, Olivia lives with her teenaged sibling, Eleanor, their odious aunt Mrs Curle, and her pompous but inoffensive son George, in a large white house overlooking the village. An acquaintance begins when the family invite Nettle to the house to play the 'cello for their amusement. Blind to their arrogance and social snobbery, and desperate to escape the home that he shares with his vulgar landlady, Mrs Clark, her slatternly teenaged daughter Pauline, and little son Alexander, Nettle aches to belong to the middle-class world of sophistication and self-confidence that for him the Nerans and Curles, and later their literary critic friend David Premiss, epitomise.

Music and form

As the titles of her books suggest, Edwards' love and extensive knowledge of music greatly influenced the style and tone of her writing and *Winter Sonata* constitutes a unique attempt to structure a work of fiction within a musical form. Perhaps this is hardly surprising given Edwards' activities when the novel had begun to take shape in her mind. "I never read!!!… I am dependant [*sic*] for inspiration entirely on concerts", she wrote to Beryl Jones in a letter from Vienna.[vi]

The novel is divided into four chapters, or movements. Edwards' use of music terms throughout the text reinforces the sense of the novel's musical composition: Olivia, for example, finds that "time seemed to move for her so slowly, like a long *adagio*" (*WS.*, 182); while for Premiss the trees and the sky "had an air of restrained gaiety like a little scherzo in a minor key" (*WS.*, 76); and Nettle has a dream that returns to him "like a chord of music" (*WS.*, 71). Words and phrases are repeated, like musical notes, to build up images in the text, particularly in relation to the landscape. As winter descends on the village and the surrounding countryside goes into hibernation, the use of a monochrome backdrop underlines the lethargic tone of the novel:

> The sky was uniformly *grey*, not *dark* with rain-clouds, but *grey* with no *white* in it anywhere. On either side of the *white* road the bare hedges and sometimes the *grey*, naked branches of a leafless tree overshadowed it a little. Some *grey* sheep moved about silently in the fields. Down in the hollow below the road, where a stream ran, the trees looked *black* and like little feathery clouds, and far upon the other side bracken lay in broad *brown* patches on the *pale*, short grass.
> (*WS.*, 21) [My emphasis.]

When colour is introduced, it is done slowly and deliberately – the green of the fir trees, the reddish streaks of a rising or setting sun. This pattern occurs from the very beginning of the novel: on Nettle's first morning in the village, at the opening of the text, the scene is described thus:

> Everywhere the trees were nearly bare, but a few golden leaves still clung to the black branches. The black curving lines and the gold leaves looked as if they were painted on the pale grey sky. (WS., 1)

This is a scene described with an artist's eye and, when describing the natural world in *Winter Sonata*, this detailed impressionistic technique is one that Edwards returns to again and again.

Images or motifs – Olivia's "large, sad eyes" (and, in fact, eyes in general), the branches of the trees, the moon, white flowers – accrue significance as they are repeated. Scenes also recur: Nettle, for example, reflects on his first meeting with Olivia several times throughout the novel. Such repetition is a key characteristic of the sonata form. The set pattern of Nettle's life, his daily walk to his job at the post office, his weekly visit to his uncle's home, and the intermittent invitations that he receives from the Neran household, always accepted, serve to add a sense of ritual and rigid form to the text. Although it encompasses a period of some months, the novel begins with the dawn of a new morning, and ends with the onset of night. *Winter Sonata* lacks the climax or conclusion integral to the traditional Victorian novel: there are no marriage proposals, no deaths, no revelations, to offer closure. Instead, it ends very much in the tone in which it began.

Women

Of the novel's characters, it is Olivia who most consistently reflects the wintry palette that forms the novel's backdrop. Emphasis is continually placed on her "round pale face" with its "large dark eyes" (*WS.*, 28), which reflect the monochrome landscape that surrounds her home. She first appears in a white woollen dress, and "[a]s she came down between the bare grey trees and along the hard grey road it was difficult to tell whether the white figure was more like summer going sadly away from the earth or like winter stealing quietly upon it" (*WS.*, 3). Passive, well-mannered, deferential, and elegant, Olivia adheres perfectly to the role of middle-class lady but, it appears, at the cost of her selfhood. Olivia's life lacks passion, drive, or purpose: she spends her time wandering aimlessly from room to room, or sitting, staring at her idle hands. Olivia embodies the winter season: associated with the fir trees which guard her door, which come to represent the unchanging, static nature of her existence; they do not participate in the seasonal change so essential to life, and contrast starkly with the bare barren skeletons, beneath which pulses the sap of life, of the deciduous trees that surround them.

Olivia's situation highlights the destructive effects of enforced passivity on the female psyche. The male characters, on the other hand, are restless and searching: George Curle is continually in pursuit of the meaning of his life, and often takes out the frustration caused by his existential angst on his mother, who cites ambition as the source of her late husband's discontent: "'he was very ambitious, and that never made him do anything out of the ordinary; it simply made him impatient,'" she tells George of his father (*WS.*, 161). Olivia, on the other hand, is aware of the value of contemplation over ambition. She says to Curle:

> "I think perhaps if one could learn to be absolutely receptive of every sensation and every impression as it comes, without any reference to what one expects, or to what one wants, one would be perfectly happy." (WS., 168)

But in her case, with no outlet of expression, her passivity results in fatigue and eventually depression. Indeed, Olivia seems to be experiencing a form of emotional hibernation as a result of the continual repression of her physical and emotional needs.

The same winter landscape, however, has a very different effect on her seventeen-year-old sister Eleanor. Fresh from school, Eleanor feels "like a bird whom no obstacle prevents from spreading its wings and flying to and fro over the earth" (*WS.*, 205). She is overjoyed to discover some snowdrops have grown in the shelter provided by the fir trees in the otherwise barren and lifeless garden. There is a suggestion that Olivia, the unchanging fir, endures her perpetual emotional and physical hibernation in part in order to protect Eleanor, represented by the snowdrops, and allow her to achieve her "spring". For as Olivia's lethargy and depression grows, Eleanor "felt very happy and gay. It seemed to her at that moment that the whole world might have been contained within herself. It made her feel as if everything around her were on the point of springing into life" (*WS.*, 218). While Eleanor and Curle admire the snowdrops enthusiastically, Olivia is dismissive, "looking down wearily at the little leaves" (*WS.*, 206), and is assailed by a wave of the depression that increasingly affects her throughout the novel:

> A sudden feeling of loneliness had come upon her, so intense, that the place and the people around her, the hard, stony garden and the trees, stood out empty and bare as though without any deeper implications, as though she had withdrawn into herself all the imagination and affection which could have given them life and depth. She felt in that moment an almost intolerable distaste for life, a kind of nausea. (WS., 207)

Protected to some extent by her elder sister, Eleanor is able to question the nature of power in society in a manner that Olivia cannot, and takes steps towards realising a female solidarity. In her penultimate encounter with Premiss, aware of his imminent departure, she engages him in a final private conversation in which, when discussing his bachelor status, he reveals his expectations of a wife's role, telling her:

"I am a very disorderly man. I have left something in every corner of the house and it takes me a terrible time to pack. It is because I am a bachelor, you know. If I had a wife it would be all right."

"But you wouldn't let your wife do your packing for you?" said Eleanor, a little shocked by this.

"Yes, I would," he said, looking at her solemnly.

"But you couldn't let your wife be a slave to you, Mr Premiss!"

"Yes, I could," he said, highly amused.

She walked on in silence.

"Why, Miss Eleanor," he said, "you are cross with me?"

"Well," she said, gravely raising her eyes to his, "if men as clever as you are willing to be among the oppressors of women, what can one expect of ordinary men?" (WS., 196-7)

Eleanor's language here is as telling as it is suggestive: not only is she being awakened to the subjugated status of women in her society, but she is beginning to realise the exploitative potential of educated middle-class men like Premiss.

Class

For the most part, however, Eleanor is blinded by her class conditioning, and this is highlighted in her interactions with her contemporary but social inferior, Pauline Clark. As the novelty of their acquaintance with Nettle wears off, the Nerans insist that he bring Pauline, the daughter of his landlady, to sing for them. Ever curious about the glamorous occupants of the white house and their privileged lifestyle, Pauline is happy to oblige and, unlike Nettle, does not confuse their patronage with friendship.

Despite her beautiful singing voice Pauline is considered by the members of the Neran household to be ignorant of the aesthetic value of her own artistic talent as a result of her class. Her torn, dog-eared songbook and the fact that she is unable to name any of the composers whose songs she sings, indicates to Eleanor and her family that Pauline is poorly educated and uncultured, and thus unqualified to appreciate artistic beauty. The same approach is extended to Nettle: in a conversation with Olivia, Eleanor says: "'you know, considering that he probably knows nothing at all about it, it seems to me he plays really rather decently'" (*WS.*, 29). Little has changed in Eleanor's attitude by the end of the novel: when handing Nettle a book of essays written by Premiss, "'You must tell us what you think of it,' she said kindly, though she did not really think that he would be able to give an opinion on it" (*WS.*, 238-9). And yet, despite her apparent vulgarity and ignorance, Pauline shows a far more incisive appreciation of music than the Nerans would credit her with. When performing in the church choir, she muses:

> It seemed to her that the organist was an old fool, but she liked to hear him play the organ. She would stop singing to hear him, and she knew she could never sing like that, like a great strong pillar reaching up to heaven. (WS., 17)

The gifts that the Neran family, and Eleanor and Olivia in particular, give to Pauline during her visits emphasise her subordinate status, and also signal her entry into a market of exchange. An initial gift of a box of chocolates is soon followed by a few drops of perfume, an orange ball gown from Olivia, and a long string of green beads that Eleanor contrives to present to Pauline, naively, in the street (*WS.*, 156). "'Thank you, *and* for the scent'", Pauline says to Olivia, gratefully enough, despite her perceived insolent nature

(*WS.*, 115). The pleasure that Pauline and her brother Alexander get from these gifts (Edwards excels when describing children) highlights their lack of material possessions. Alexander is overawed by the mysterious gifts that his sister brings home, despite their overtly feminine nature: when he sees Pauline in the orange dress "his wonder made his eyes wider and wider", and the following day he continually peeps into a trunk where Pauline hides the dress for fear of reprisal from her mother (*WS.*, 116-7,118). The scent, too, occasions a similar reaction in Alexander; when Pauline gives him the perfume-drenched handkerchief, he "smelt it, looking up at her over it, and when she began to take it away he put his hand up to keep it there for still another moment" (*WS.*, 117).

Pauline is by far the most overtly sexual of Edwards' women, and is unabashedly intrigued by the opposite sex. When her attempts to flirt with Nettle are met with an embarrassed confusion, she instead makes use of him as an unwitting aid to her late-night escapades with the local choirboys:

> On choir-practice nights, as soon as the clock struck seven, even if she were in the middle of some work, she would put everything down and run across to the church [...] After the practice she ran out of the churchyard like a little cat and walked slowly up the road pretending she liked to take a walk by herself [...] in winter it was already dark, and almost before she turned the corner she could walk slowly, and some of the boys would follow her [.]...More than once, when he [Nettle] was getting ready to go up [to bed], he heard Pauline's light tap on the window. He pulled up the blind and she signed to him to let her in. (WS., 16-7, 24)

The arrival of Mr Premiss, whom she finds even more fascinating than her choirboys, offers Pauline a new object for her
attentions, and she frequently abandons her domestic duties
in order to intercept him on his early-morning walks. But
Premiss, who sees himself as something of a daring flirt, is
curiously void of passion during his encounters with Pauline.
Like Nettle, Premiss is depicted as a strangely desexualized,
ineffective, male, and, "rather short and exceedingly pale",
his physical appearance is suggestive of a lack of vigour and
strength (*WS.*, 72). Premiss appears driven by anthropological interest rather than by any sexual urge, and he relishes the
irony of the situations Pauline finds herself in. When she
sings for the family, for example, "[i]t gave him immense
pleasure to hear the voice of Bach's Virgin come from
Pauline's lips" (*WS.*, 112). Premiss likens Pauline's temperament to that of a Bacchante, emphasising his view of her as
an overly sexualized and physical, not intellectual, being
(*WS.*, 121).

Edwards' treatment of Pauline is sympathetic as well as rig-
orous. Pauline is depicted as uncouth, undisciplined, curious,
insolent and lazy, but she is judged entirely by the social stan-
dards of others and there is an underlying suggestion that
Pauline is merely a misunderstood young woman. Her insolent
half smile, for example, could be as a result of shyness:
"Pauline smiled up at… [Curle] in her rather insolent way. It
may have been from gratitude" (*WS.*, 179). Pauline's attention
seeking may be an attempt to replace the lack of affection
shown to her by her mother, and her interest in the Neran
sisters and their clothing an escape from the drab and punish-
ing routine of her working-class life. Pauline is desperately
lacking a father figure (the loss of Edwards' father perhaps
offers a model here): the absence of Pauline's father is a source
pain and discomfort to her mother, whose comments suggest
that this is the result of some sexual misconduct. "You mark
my words; you'll get into trouble some day […] you're like

your father, that's what you are", says Mrs Clark to Pauline
after seeing her with Premiss (*WS*, 129).

Pauline's relationship with her mother is volatile and
explosive; verbally and physically abusive, it is very different from the strained and tense but always stifling propriety
of the middle-class relationships that characterise Edwards'
fiction. This is the only mother-daughter relationship in
Edwards' oeuvre; it is as startling as it is telling in its com-
plexity and may well owe something to Edwards'
relationship with her own mother. Like Pauline, Edwards felt
that she was constantly harangued over domestic tasks:
"From morning to night I am likely at any moment to be
rowed – though not very ferociously – for anything," she said
in a letter to college friend Sona Rosa Burstein.[viii]

Despite their poverty and perceived vulgarity, the Clarks'
way of life is ultimately presented as natural and healthy in
comparison to the continual self-repression endured by the
occupants of the Neran household. Pauline and Alexander
consistently act on their instincts without fear of reprisal or
social consequences: in the opening scene of the novel, for
example, little Alexander, deceived by the unseasonable
warmth of a mild day in early winter, "took off his dress in
the middle of the road" (*WS.*, 2). By virtue of their class,
then, Eleanor and Olivia appear prevented from expressing
such genuine human feeling and emotion in the way that
Pauline does. A physical and emotional existence, it appears,
is ultimately far less stultifying than a cultured but repressive
middle-class lifestyle.

Isolation and loneliness

Although Pauline and her family inject some vigour into the
novel, the overwhelming impression that remains is that of
lethargy, of hibernation, as its title suggests. There are no
heroes in this novel. Edwards' characters suffer from isolation
and loneliness as well as various forms of debilitating depres-

sion, like that increasingly coming to dominate her own life at the time of the novel's writing. Nettle is lonely and longing for a world from which he is excluded. Olivia suffers from lethargy and depression that she conceals from her family; George is continually seeking a sense of self-worth, while Pauline longs for loving attention and comfort but receives scorn and abuse instead. Even Premiss is an isolated man: he puts on a charismatic front when in company, but he dislikes being alone at night and suffers from insomnia.

Fascinatingly, Edwards was apparently unaware of the isolated positions in which she placed her characters when writing. A letter to David Garnett, following a visit to him in 1931, shows her reaction when rereading her own work:

> When I got home, first of all I read *Winter Sonata* to see if anything in it justified all the kindness people had shown me, and I must confess that I could hardly read through it […] it is so bleak and cold that I nearly got frostbite while I read, and the chief thing it portrays is an awful emptiness, very distressing to have to read about.ii

At first glance a typical 'English' novel about middle-class life, *Winter Sonata* is in fact a deeply unsettling account of the iniquity that Edwards perceived in her society and, ultimately, the unassailable loneliness of the human soul.

NOTES

[i] Dorothy Edwards Archive (MS5085), University of Reading, Special Collections (hereafter DEA); packet 6. Dorothy Edwards, diary entry, n.d. [1933].

[ii] DEA; packet 6. Dorothy Edwards, diary entry, n.d. [1933].

[iii] An entry in the Tynewydd Schools Logbook on 22 January 1918 states: "Mrs Vida Edwards commenced duties", and on 31 March 1919: "Mrs Vida Edwards has been transferred to Ely (nr Cardiff) School." Glamorgan Archives, Tynewydd Schools Logbook (E/M/55/6), 22 January 1918, 119, and 31 March 1919, 131.

[iv] Dorothy Edwards, letter to S. Beryl Jones and Winifred Kelly, n.d. [c.1928-1932]. DEA, packet 5, item 19.

[v] Dorothy Edwards, letter to Sona Rosa Burstein, 30th August [c. 1930-32]. DEA, packet 3, item 30.

[vi] DEA; packet 5, item 5. Dorothy Edwards, letter to S. Beryl Jones, n.d. [c.1926].

[vii] Dorothy Edwards, letter to Sona Rosa Burstein, 30th August n.d. DEA, packet 3, item 30.

[viii] Dorothy Edwards, letter to David Garnett, 1st June 1931. Garnett Family Archive, Charles Deering McCormick Library of Special Collections, Northwestern University Library Courtesy of Richard Garnett.

Hât der Winter kurzen tac
sô hat her die langen naht
daz sich liep bî liebe mac
wol erholn, daz ê dâ vaht.
Waz hân ich gesprochen? ôwé jâ
haete ich baz geswigen
sol ich iemer sô geligen.

WALTER VON DER VOGELWEIDE
(Lob des Winters).

CHAPTER 1

It was a beautifully fine day; the sun shone and it was warm. Everyone who had time hurried out in case it should be the last warm day before winter came. Mr Arnold Nettle, the new telegraph clerk, stood for a few minutes outside his lodgings before he walked to the post-office. He had a long, thin neck and looked rather delicate, and he was in fact ill and had come to work here so as to escape winter in the town. He had arrived only the night before. It had been cold and rainy and depressing, but now on the first day here it was beautiful, as if to welcome him. Everywhere the trees were nearly bare, but a few golden leaves still clung to the black branches. The black curving lines and the gold leaves looked as if they were painted on the pale grey sky. The sun shone quite warmly through thin clouds, but the earth had already hardened itself for winter, and did not respond.

Only the children and the cats in the village were deceived by the warmth. Little Alexander Clark, the little boy at Mr Nettle's lodgings, took off his dress in the middle of the road. His sister Pauline, when she saw it, slapped him until he cried. She put his dress on him again, always holding him firmly by one arm and shaking him every now and then, so that his sobs came in jerks. Then she left him to sit on the edge of the pavement. Somebody who passed gave him a halfpenny to stop crying, but the little boy from next door took it away from him when they were out of sight, and Alexander, still crying, started going up the road for a walk by himself.

His sister Pauline went to the post-office. She was supposed to be shopping for her mother, but she wanted to see the new lodger first. He had come late last night, and this morning her mother would not let her take his breakfast in but did it herself. She went in and asked for a telegraph form. Arnold Nettle gave it to her. He was a strange young man, and much better dressed than any of the choir-boys. She smiled at him, and then looked down at her feet and began scraping one of them on the floor. She looked up again as if she could not help laughing. Nettle evidently thought she was laughing at him. He blushed. It appears that he was very shy, and he had, besides, a nameless fear of girls.

The tops of the tallest trees were already quite bare of leaves; they stretched out against the grey sky. Farther up, on the hill, three little fir trees stood up in front of a white house. Against the whiteness of the walls they looked a deep green. Olivia, the elder of the two sisters who lived there, came down the hill in a white woollen dress. As she came down between the bare grey trees and along the hard grey road it was difficult to tell whether the white figure was more like summer going sadly away from the earth or like winter stealing quietly upon it.

Pauline turned round to look after her as she passed, though she was not interested of course in any symbolic significance that might have been attached to her, but only in her dress. Both the Neran sisters always had nice dresses, and they were moreover pretty. Olivia had a round pale face and large, rather sad eyes, and her eyelashes curved right up, giving her a childlike and innocent look. As she went past the post-office, Arnold Nettle happened to see her through the window. He turned his long thin neck to look at her, and when she had gone out of sight he sat down at his table again and blushed a little to himself.

But in the evening, after this fine day, the wind rose and big grey clouds floated through the sky. Gusts of wind came tearing through the village, beating at doors and windows, and making the branches of the trees rattle together horribly. It blew like that all night, and by the morning all the golden leaves had been torn from the bare trees, and they lay on the cold hard earth and in the roads beneath the horses' feet and the wheels of cars. The wind was cold and biting. Winter had come.

It sometimes happens that when we go to a new place from which we expect a great deal we pick out from the new faces there one which seems to us a guarantee of the possibility of all that we hope for from it, and it is probably for a reason something like this that Arnold Nettle more than once remembered Olivia walking past in the white dress on his first day in the village, and recalled everything about her as vividly as if she could possibly have been the herald for him of some sort of step towards health, which was after all the only reason for his coming here. When, a few days afterwards, she came to the post-office to send a telegram, one might almost say that he felt excited. She asked him for a form, and the curious thing was that he was not very shy. He looked at her with his head held a little awkwardly, and he smiled and gave her one. She did not notice him, but she took the form and began to feel the points of the pens against the tip of her finger. He looked into the ink-well and fetched some ink to pour in, and he spilt some and had to wipe it up with blotting-paper. She helped him to do this. It all took place just as in a dream; his hand did not knock against hers, of if it did, he moved it away quite naturally without feeling embarrassed. He counted the words wrongly, and she had to correct him, and he did not mind this either, but said, "Oh yes, excuse me," and she smiled and nodded.

As she went out she turned her head to look over her shoulder, and said, "Will it go at once?"

And he smiled now and said perfectly naturally, "Yes, certainly it shall."

Afterwards he felt that everything had not perhaps gone quite so smoothly. The ink had, after all, been spilt, and there were many little things not quite right: it was foolish to have counted the words wrongly. But for a long time afterwards he felt excited and happy, and there was the feeling of certainty that, as a matter of fact, everything had been quite without a flaw. But ordinarily in himself he was terribly shy.

The two Neran girls had always lived with their uncle in the white house with the fir trees, but he had died the year before, and now an aunt had come to live with them. The uncle was their mother's brother; this aunt was the sister of their father. She used to walk about the village, shopping. She was rather fat, and also she looked a bit like a goose, and just as a goose looks cruel in a stupid way she had that expression too. She did not like living in the country very much, but it had not occurred to her to refuse to come and live with her nieces. Her son had come with her, a dark, fat little man, very good-natured and amiable. He said that he was studying philosophy, and often had an air of extreme importance.

If this Mrs Curle ever saw anybody in the village who, she believed, could entertain her in any way she hurriedly made his acquaintance. When she saw the new clerk in the post-office she inquired if he had only just come. The post-master was his uncle – that is why he had chosen to come particularly there. He called him, and he had to get up from his table and come to speak to her through the railing. He blushed and smiled awkwardly and stammered answers to her questions. She looked at him without smiling, and shook hands with him rather absent-mindedly, but when she went home she remarked that he looked intelligent.

He had brought with him a cello when he came to the village; he could play it, and he used to practise it in his lodgings. He bent his long neck over it and looked at the music propped up on a chair in front of him. The organist at the church was a friend of his uncle, and when he heard that he could play he asked him to perform at some social that was to be held in the church hall. Nettle did not like to say no, though he began to tremble with nervousness almost immediately.

The church was exactly opposite where he lived, and he was just carrying the cello across the road for a practice when he met Mrs Curle and her son. They were going through the village for a walk. The evening was just beginning. Mrs Curle walked along slowly, looking in front of her, and she went past Mr Nettle, but then, evidently because the form of the cello had impressed itself on her mind, she stopped and looked back. She took hold of her son's arm to bring him with her and returned a few paces.

"Here is Mr Nettle," she said.

George Curle looked rather surprised, but smiled at him amiably.

"Do you play that?" she asked.

Holding the cello in a tight embrace, Mr Nettle smiled, and said, "Yes."

"We are going for a walk," began George Curle conversationally, but his mother interrupted him and said urgently, "You must come up some evening to play to us. What time does the post-office shut?"

"Six o'clock," said Mr Nettle.

"I will send and let you know which day," she said, beginning to walk on.

George Curle smiled good-bye and then followed her.

Mr Nettle looked after them in some astonishment, because he did not quite know what to think, then he opened the churchyard gate and went round to the hall behind the church.

Not very long afterwards she sent a message down to the post-office to ask him to come up to see them that evening. He was rather shy at going there. But there was no question of refusing. He put on his best suit, took his cello, and walked slowly up the hill to their house. About half-way he began to have a sort of feeling of alarm, which could not be explained. But since he could not very well change his mind and go back, he walked the rest of the way very quickly. He went in through the gate, and when he reached the door he was still out of breath and he stood for a moment to regain it before ringing. The shadow of one of the little fir trees fell in the moonlight across the door.

The door suddenly opened, even before he had rung. Dazzled a little by the sudden light, he stood blinking into the hall.

"Here you are," said George Curle. "I heard the gate."

He led him into the drawing-room. Olivia and Eleanor were there, and Mrs Curle was sitting with a cat on her lap.

Mr Nettle smiled shyly at them all and fixed his eyes on the cat, and stood awkwardly while George Curle put a chair for him.

"That chair won't do," said Mrs Curle, "it's too low."

"Is it too low for you?" asked Eleanor, putting her book down on the table and looking up at him with interest. He looked at her shyly. She was very young, almost a schoolgirl, but all the same he was a little embarrassed at so much solicitude. He shyly nodded.

George Curle got another and put it for him. Nettle sat down and took the cover off the cello, and then let it lie on the floor in front of him. He was conscious that they were all looking at him, so he did not raise his eyes from the ground. But Eleanor spoke to him.

"Do you like it here?" she asked, looking at him with her blue eyes. "Auntie says you have only just come."

He darted one glance at her, and then said "Yes," and looked down at the carpet again.

"You know, to me this place is very puzzling," said George Curle, standing in the middle of the room and with his hands in his pockets, pulling his coat tightly around him, and, although this made him look a little ridiculous, preserving an air of great gravity on his face, as though he knew that he was going to say something really amusing. "I must first of all admit that I am no botanist; I could never in my life tell the difference between a pine and a fir tree. To-day, when I was out, I saw a big fir tree or pine tree growing between two houses, and one house was called Pine Lodge, so I thought, 'Well, here I am, I know at last'; and then I came to the next house, and that was called The Firs, so I was just where I started from."

Olivia laughed, and Mr Nettle could hear her saying in her soft voice, "But, George, you have been living here for nearly a year, and it is disgraceful that you do not realise that we have three fir trees in the garden."

"Is that so, really," said George; "then my doubts are solved."

He began to stroke the cat on his mother's lap. There was a little silence as if they were all expecting Mr Nettle to say something, but he still looked at the carpet and would have been quite unable to find anything to say.

Mrs Curle had a definite distaste for conversation; she herself sat most of the time without making more than a few remarks, and, what was rather funny, she always tried to interrupt the conversation of other people and make them all do something instead, so that it seemed to her that Mr Nettle was a very sensible man to sit there without speaking until he was asked to play. But the others felt that it was a little awkward not to be able to get a word out of him at all.

"Why doesn't Olivia play something?" said Mrs Curle in a rather aggrieved voice.

Olivia went to the piano, and Nettle, who had not been able to look at her before, watched her very intently all the time that she was playing. Afterwards they played together. He was very nervous that he would not play it properly, but they went through it all right.

George Curle thanked him very much, and Eleanor looked

at him with much more interest; but now that the conversation had begun again, Mrs Curle was staring intently at the top of the window curtain, where there was a large spider.

After they had played again, Eleanor brought them tea. Nettle put his cello down on the floor and took the little Japanese cup from her hand. It was so thin that one could see through it to where the tea came. He held it with both his hands, until Olivia saw it and put a little table at his side for him to put it on. He smiled at her, but she had turned away already. He kept looking at the little cup; one often breaks things of that kind, especially if one feels nervous about them. There was a Japanese lady in yellow upon it. He kept looking at her, and then he drank his tea over the thin edge. The other people in the room talked, and if they said anything to him, he smiled at them but he did not talk. He bent down to stroke the cat that came and rubbed against the leg of his chair, purring loudly, its tail standing up in the air. He looked up again: Olivia was looking at him.

"Is there anyone else in the village who can play or do anything?" asked Mrs Curle abruptly.

"The organist at the church can play," said Nettle, glad to be able to answer this direct question.

"I know him," she said. "He always asks me to go to church to hear his choir, but I don't like going to church."

She looked at Nettle, and he smiled with a little embarrassment; then suddenly realising that he was expected to give an answer to this too, he said, "But there is a little boy in the choir who has a beautiful voice. I have heard him practising. He sings like an angel. I think you would like to hear him. He is going to sing a solo on Sunday morning."

"Oh," said Mrs Curle. "Is there anyone else?"

Mr Nettle looked rather alarmed. "The daughter of my landlady has a voice," he said; "she is going to sing at the church social."

"Is she pretty?" asked Mrs Curle.

He did not seem to think it necessary to answer.

"What is she like?" asked Eleanor. "We probably know her."

"I don't know," said Mr Nettle doubtfully.

"You don't know what she is like?" said George Curle laughing.

Mr Nettle smiled. "Her mother says she has a lot of trouble with her; she says she is flighty."

George laughed, and Olivia smiled at him with her large, rather sad eyes.

They did not play any more before he went home. He carried the cello down the hill; there was a bright moon, but there were many clouds in the sky; big grey clouds moving slowly across, so that there were no stars. The little fir trees stood out against the white house and one could tell that they were very green even at night like this. Nettle walked slowly down the hill carrying the cello in his arms.

When he got back to his lodgings he opened the door quietly and went in. The house was in darkness, because it was quite late. Just as he had shut the door behind him he heard hurried footsteps on the pavement and a light tap at the door. He opened it again, and saw Pauline Clark standing outside.

"Hush," she said, quietly pushing herself in through the half-opened door and shutting it again without a sound. "I saw you going in, and I ran," she said, sitting down on the stairs to regain her breath and pulling her dress down over her knees. "I didn't want to come in through the back, because my mother'd hear me, and I'd catch it for being out late. If I can get undressed before she sees me, I can say I've been in a long time. I lost my garter, so I had to hold up my stocking all the way home."

She scarcely looked at Mr Nettle as she whispered, because she was preoccupied with listening for sounds from upstairs.

"Where have you been?" he whispered back.

"Out!" she said. "Don't you tell her."

She took off her shoes and went quietly up the stairs to her room. There was some of her leg showing between her dress and the stocking. She had stopped holding it up. The house was quite still. Nettle went up to his room very quietly, and read for a bit before he went to sleep.

Pauline had found, after all, that Mr Nettle was not very interesting, and for this reason she made him useful. It was more fun to go round with the choir-boys. On choir practice-nights, as soon as the clock struck seven, even if she were in the middle of some work, she would put everything down and run across to the church. Her mother shouted after her from the kitchen, but she took no notice. She looked up and down the road to see if anyone was coming, and then went in smiling through the gate. In the church porch she walked about pretending to read the notices on the door and on the walls at the side, but she knew that the boys were looking at her.

They went in to sing. She sang better than any of the other girls. It seemed to her that the organist was an old fool, but she liked to hear him play the organ. She would stop singing to hear him, and she knew she could never sing like that, like a great strong pillar reaching up to heaven.

After the practice she ran out of the churchyard like a little cat and walked slowly up the road pretending she liked to take a walk by herself. In the summer it was still light, and her mother watched for her from the house, and she had to go in if she was not careful. But in winter it was already dark, and almost before she turned the corner she could walk slowly, and some of the boys would follow her. They shouted things after her and threw little stones, and she never bothered to turn round. But if their shouting and laughing stopped, and she could not hear them coming behind her, then she looked round and she smiled a bit scornfully and as though she wanted to laugh. When she turned to come home, they walked along together, the boys grinning like idiots, and she did not know what to say to them either, but she always smiled a bit scornfully as if they were not worth talking to.

When she got in, her mother would give her a row, but she shrugged her shoulders and escaped as soon as she could up to bed. Little Alexander, who slept with her, would sleep all night without moving, and she would lie looking at the shadows on the ceiling of her room until she fell asleep too. Sometimes she was frightened to think that if anything were to happen in the churchyard in the middle of the night she would see the shadows on her wall, because it was so near, but by the morning she had forgotten it. Her mother came to wake her so early that it was still dark. Often she had to be dragged out of bed; she hated being awakened. She would have liked to push little Alexander, sleeping calmly with his mouth open, out of bed. She went downstairs and did the work she had to do, but she sulked all the morning. She sulked until there was a chance to go out to the shop and see people. She would stay out as long as she dared, and when she got home her mother would give it to her, call her "a huzzy; a good-for-nothing; a slut."

She was always interested in the people up at the Nerans' house; if ever Olivia or Eleanor passed, she would go out on the street to see what they were wearing.

One Sunday morning she was standing outside seeing that Alexander did not dirty his best clothes when Mrs Curle and George Curle passed.

He looked at her and said something to his mother. Pauline laughed across at him and turned round and looked again over her shoulder. He came across the road to speak to her.

"Does Mr Nettle stay in your house?" he asked.

"Yes," she said smiling.

He went back to his mother. "Yes, that is she," he said.

Mrs Curle looked at her with a kind of irritated attention, but why she should have been irritated no one knew.

Arnold Nettle, coming at this moment along the road, failing to catch Mrs Curle's eye and encountering only the back of her son, who had turned round and was looking up the hill, stood smiling shyly at her elbow, for he felt that it was his duty to speak to them and had not the desperate courage to begin. She relinquished her interest in the girl and turned round abruptly to find him standing very near her and smiling, by this time in an agony of embarrassment.

"Are you going to church?" she asked with some severity.

"No," said Nettle.

"I haven't been to church for ten years," she said, "and I hate it on Sunday mornings; but I am going to hear your choir-boy."

Nettle smiled and looked at her, but did not say anything.

The church bells began to ring.

"Where are you going?" asked George Curle.

"For a walk, I think," said Nettle.

"Then I can come with you," he said.

Mrs Curle began to walk in through the gate of the churchyard.

"It's early," said Nettle.

"I came early to get a good seat," she said, without looking round; and they could see her going to sit down on the bench in the porch to wait for the doors to open. She was, it seemed, under the impression that going to church was a very popular pastime.

George Curle laughed in a pleased way, and said, "She talks as if she were going to a theatre. You know," he added, "I consider her in many ways a very original woman; don't you agree?"

"Yes," said Nettle, who really thought so.

They walked along the road. The sky was uniformly grey, not dark with rain-clouds, but grey with no white in it any-where. On either side of the white road the bare hedges and sometimes the grey, naked branches of a leafless tree overshadowed it a little. Some grey sheep moved about silently in the fields. Down in the hollow below the road, where a stream ran, the trees looked black and like little feathery clouds, and far upon the other side bracken lay in broad brown patches on the pale, short grass.

George Curle walked along kicking a stone in front of him and whistling almost inaudibly, the top and lower notes of the tune not audible at all. Nettle walked at his side, and whenever there came a gust of wind his hand went up hastily to hold his hat.

"What do you think of my cousins?" said George Curle.

Nettle smiled shyly but did not find anything to say.

"Do you think they are pretty?" continued George Curle.

"Yes," said Nettle decidedly.

"Which do you think is the prettier?"

"The dark one."

"Oh, Olivia," said George Curle in surprise. "Do you really? Most people find Eleanor very beautiful."

Nettle shook his head.

"I think the dark one is very beautiful," he repeated with decision, and then blushed.

"Of course Eleanor is only a child," said George thoughtfully, "and I understand your preferring mature beauty to something merely potential, but you know everybody agrees that when she is a year or two older she will really be a quite striking beauty, something that you do not meet every day. Don't you think so?"

Nettle nodded.

"You know, I am awfully attached to them," said George Curle confidentially. "I shall be awfully sorry if they ever go away from us, get married or something. We have been living here with them ever since their uncle died. They are both very young, of course, and have not much experience of life," he said, kicking his stone along the road, "but you have no idea what good comrades they make."

Nettle smiled. They did not take a very long walk, but turned back soon. And they did not talk much, because Nettle was not the man to begin a subject of conversation, and George Curle's amiable remarks did not call urgently for answers; but after this George Curle always felt that he knew Nettle very well.

When they got back to the village Nettle stopped at the post-office because he was going to have dinner with his uncle. George Curle went on alone. The people were still in church; when he reached there he could hear them singing. So he went and sat down on the bench in the porch, and resting his cheek on his hand, listened to the singing and waited for his mother.

Every evening at six o'clock Arnold Nettle used to come home from the post-office and walk slowly along to his lodgings. The sun was setting, and it would disappear behind the black feathery branches of the trees, leaving streaks of red in the grey sky. He went in and had his tea, and then he usually sat reading by the fire or practising a bit on his cello. Sometimes, of course, he sat simply looking into the fire, and it seemed that he was a little nervous even in his own society, because often he would begin to blush and smile shyly to himself. At ten o'clock he would put his book and his cello back in their places and fasten the window and go to bed.

More than once, when he was getting ready to go up, he heard Pauline's light tap on the window. He pulled up the blind and she signed to him to let her in. He went out into the passage and opened the door very quietly. When she came in she was often out of breath through running, but she tried even to breathe quietly. She nodded her thanks for his con-nivance, and brushing close against him made her way quietly upstairs. He looked up after her, and at the top she turned round and smiled at him. She had the same irritating expression on her face of wanting to laugh.

"She certainly is flighty," he thought to himself, and opening the door again, he looked out into the street to see if there was anyone there. No one was about; there was a new moon in the sky. He went in, thinking that perhaps he ought to tell her mother. It was very unlikely though that he ever would.

When he had shut and locked the door there was no longer anyone to be seen. The sharp sickle of the moon shone coldly, and thin white clouds moved in cold silence across the sky. There were no stars, and if there had been, there was nothing for them to see with their cold cunning little eyes. The square tower of the church stood silent in the darkness; if its clock struck, the sound seemed to cut the air like a sharp cold knife and the silence closed up again after it. The tower leaned, wrapped in its dark shadows, over the churchyard and the cold graves. A tall yew tree, disturbed by the wind, rapped continually against the roof of the little gateway. But farther down, beyond the little church, the water in the brook flowed noisily under the dark sky; it went right beneath the empty white road, which stretched far away beyond it. Above, the black branches of a tree reached far upwards. Everything stood immovable; nothing could break the hard winter stillness. The clock on the church tower struck off the hours, but the night seemed to stand still. Then suddenly there were scraps of red in the lighter sky, the sun came up behind grey clouds, and it was morning already.

Sheep began to move about slowly in the fields. The last bit of redness faded out of the sky, and the sun shone with a strong white light behind the grey clouds. A biting east wind blew through the village, and the bare branches of the trees rattled together. The fir trees, holding the dark green of their branches against the grey sky, rustled as if it were still summer, but, as it were, with hoarse voices. At the top of some high trees at the roadside were the old nests of the rooks, like small grey balls of cloud caught in the tangle of the branches. The wind blew in waves over the short pale grass of a field. Here and there in it were patches of reddish brown, and around it in the distance the low, leafless hedges looked like little banks of black smoke which had rolled away from the field itself. Great white clouds drifted slowly across the grey sky. The hard white light moved like a ghost over the clouds as the sun climbed invisibly upwards.

At midday this light, and not the warm sun itself, shone coldly, and then the haunted sun began its downward climb, until a long strip of red showed that it had set, and the white light grew harder and brighter and spread itself along the black line of the hill. Then it slowly faded out, dragging pale, purple-grey clouds after it to the horizon.

The moon came again, but now its sharp edges were blurred and a few stars had appeared here and there in the sky. The wind had fallen, and the trees stretched out their dark branches motionlessly in the cold air.

The morning light scarcely let its coming be seen, for the dawn screened itself behind a drizzling cold thin rain. The people went about like grey shadows through the rain. It lasted until midday, but in the afternoon it cleared off, and the sky was full of white clouds floating swiftly across it, far above the wet fields.

It was Saturday; Arnold Nettle walked through the village in his mackintosh and began to stroll up the hill towards Olivia's house. He was not intending to call there, of course, he was only going for a walk. The road was dark grey after the rain; there had been no sun since then to dry it. On the little black branches in the hedges cold raindrops still hung. Nettle came near to the house; he looked up at it once or twice, at the closed door and the fir trees in the garden, but when the little fir trees no longer hid the windows he walked on without casting on it even a casual glance.

If Olivia had been standing at the window he would not have seen her, but she could easily have seen him walking along knocking his walking-stick against the toe of his boot and looking at the ground. He went on, though, much farther and he thought quite often of how she had looked on the day when she came to send the telegram, and she looked over her shoulder to say good-bye as she went out, or rather not to say good-bye, but to ask if the telegram would go at once; and he had said, "Yes, certainly, at one," or something like that, while he looked at her round pale face and her large dark eyes.

When he turned back it was still light on the hill, but down in the valley one could see that it was already night. When he had passed the house he turned and looked back at it; the doorway was almost invisible in the shadow of the fir trees.

He began to think it would be nothing extraordinary if he were to go to the door and ask if he had left some music there by mistake; he did not intend to go in, but only to knock at the door and ask that. He was on the way back from a walk, and it had only just occurred to him as he was passing the house that the piece of music which had been lost for some time might perhaps be there. It was rather a good idea, but it was very unlikely that he would put it into action. He went on walking while he thought of it, and he reached the bottom of the hill without turning back at all.

It happened that Olivia and Eleanor were actually walking in the garden when Mr Nettle passed, but they came to the front of the house again only when he was already far down the hill. They could see his back, rather bent because he was evidently looking at his shoes.

"Look," said Olivia, "it's Mr Nettle."

"Is it?" said Eleanor, stopping to look and laughing. "What an extraordinary mackintosh."

The mackintosh was in fact a little peculiar; it was very wide and had a deep yoke at the back.

Olivia smiled. "He is rather nice though, don't you think so?" she said.

"Oh yes," said Eleanor, "and you know, considering that he probably knows nothing at all about it, it seems to me he plays really rather decently." She put her arm through Olivia's to keep her from going on, and they stood looking at Nettle until he went out of sight. Then they walked on together round into the shadows of the little fir trees and behind the house.

"I think it is rather nice of George to take such a fancy to him," said Olivia, still smiling at the thought of Nettle's back in the peculiar mackintosh.

Eleanor laughed. "Oh, but he says a philosopher doesn't mind from whom he extracts truth; only it seems to me he would have to be clever if he even extracted conversation out of Mr Nettle."

They came round again to the grass in front of the house. It was now quite dark. The lights had been on for a long time indoors and shone through the branches of the fir trees on to the garden.

The front door opened, and George Curle came out.

"Hullo, why don't you come in?" he said, coming towards them. "You will catch cold. What secrets have you been talking?"

Eleanor went to the other side of him and put her arm through his.

"About love," she said laughing.

"Have you?" said George Curle doubtfully.

"Yes, really," she said. "We have been saying what kind of husbands we should like. Haven't we, Olivia?"

Olivia did not answer.

"Have you indeed?" asked George, rather interested. He turned to Olivia. "Is it true?"

"No," she said; "we weren't talking of anything in particular."

"Oh," said George reproachfully.

"If you want to know very badly what my ideal is," said

Eleanor, "I will tell you, but first you must, of course, tell me what is your ideal."

George smiled, rather pleased at the turn the conversation was taking.

"That is a subject which requires much consideration," he said, beginning to walk towards the house.

"Oh, I can wait while you consider," said Eleanor, suddenly taking her arm away from his and running towards the fir trees. She held a branch bent around her shoulders and stood there laughing.

George and Olivia stood smiling at her.

"If you stay out in the cold like this you will get ill and go off into consumption and be nobody's ideal," said George.

"But that is considered very attractive," she said, "like the Lady of the Camellias."

"All right, then we shall leave you to it," said George, putting his hands in the pocket of his coat and turning on his heel. And he and Olivia went in.

Eleanor looked after them, and then she drew the branch of the fir tree more closely around her and looked at the sky. It was now quite dark except just above the horizon where the sun had set. She stood there quite quietly and thought for a considerable time about various important things, and then she turned to go in.

In Mr Nettle's house very early in the morning, when it was still dark, Pauline's mother came in to call her. She did not want to wake little Alexander too, so she shook Pauline without saying anything. Pauline turned her head on the pillow and opened her eyes heavily. Her mother was just going out of the door. She got up from bed, and began, half-asleep, to dress in the dark, but then, yawning, she went to the window and pushed the curtain aside. The clock on the church tower was striking. It was beginning to grow lighter, but the day looked grey and heavy. She looked at Alexander sleeping on the bed, and wondered sulkily to herself why he should have the privilege of lying there longer. She could not stop herself from giving him a rather savage pinch.

He must have felt it, but he did not actually awaken. She went down quietly, pulling on her dress on the way downstairs. She fetched a torn pinafore from the kitchen and drank a cup of tea. Then sulkily, and still yawning, she went to clear out the grate in Mr Nettle's room.

She sat down and began to clear the ashes, but she got up again to draw up the blind. Some people were walking along the street, but it was too dark still to make it interesting to look out. When she had cleared the ashes she began almost without knowing it to read the serial story in the newspaper with which she was supposed to be laying the new fire, and gradually she became more awake.

When her mother came in to lay Mr Nettle's breakfast she was still reading. She suddenly felt the paper snatched out of her hand and knocked against her head. She looked up a little dazed and astonished, and then sulkily shrugged her shoulders. Her mother looked down at her in a fury.

"I'll turn you out of the house, you lazy little slut," she said.

Pauline shrugged her shoulders again, and got up from the floor. She was used to this sort of thing, but this morning she was in a bit of a temper already, so she answered, "I can go myself without that," and with a sulky smile she began to walk out of the room.

Her mother gave her a violent push which sent her flying through the door into the passage. This put her into a furious temper. She ran to the kitchen, flung her pinafore on the floor, and ran out through the door. Her mother came to the kitchen window and called her back with threats and names. Pauline laughed, turned her back on her, and went out of the gate. She began to walk down the road, not in the least knowing in which direction to go. She was rather cold, because she had no coat. It was already quite light; there were more people about. She began to walk up the hill slowly, although it was cold. She felt angry and walked along looking downwards and with her lips pressed sulkily together. It had rained a little in the night. The road was grey with the rain, and the grey and black branches of the bare trees were wet. All the dust from the hedges had been washed off, and only little drops of water remained hanging on to the ends of the twigs, not glistening in the sun, but grey too under the dull sky. Pauline went up the hill a long way, and though she felt sulky for some time, at last she began to lose all sensation of anger, and since it was very cold and she wanted her breakfast, she turned and walked quickly back, smiling at anyone she happened to meet.

While Mr Nettle was having breakfast, Mrs Clark told him about her daughter and how worried she was over her wickedness. Nettle drank his tea guiltily and thought that the moment had come for him to have to tell how often he had opened the door for her to come in late, but he did not open his mouth about it after all.

"She'll come to a bad end," said her mother, beginning absent-mindedly in her desperation to gather the breakfast-things together with her long thin hands, before Nettle had finished. "What can I do with her?" she said. "When she isn't in a sulky fit she can work as well as anyone. If she went out somewhere to service her sulks wouldn't do her any good, but if she were to go out of my sight there'd soon be some trouble or other." She stopped and looked at Nettle with a hard, anxious expression on her face.

"She is a bit flighty," said Nettle, wishing to give some support and knowing that this adjective could not offend since he had learned it from Mrs Clark herself.

She put the things which she had picked up from the table down again with a bang and said, "Flighty? She's a brazen huzzy. I'll beat her within an inch of her life when she comes home."

Nettle went on drinking his tea. Mrs Clark looked out through the window, and then turned away and went out of the room.

In the kitchen Alexander was waiting for his breakfast. His mother drew the loaf of bread across the table towards her and began cutting it without looking at him. She gave him a big slice and a cup of milk, and he began eating, looking at her with large not very much astonished eyes. Tears began to follow each other down her cheeks, though they were occasionally displaced by a spasm of anger which compressed her thin lips and wrinkled her forehead. Alexander seeing this, made use of the opportunity of being unobserved to lick the butter off his bread and then to put some jam on in its place.

The latch of the door was lifted and Pauline came in smiling rather uncertainly. She went to warm her hands at the fire. Her mother said nothing, and did not so much as look up at her. Alexander sat quietly on his chair and drank his milk, looking over the edge of the cup from his sister to his mother, and he did not think it wise to move, even when the milk was gone.

Pauline came to the table and took what breakfast she could without asking for the rest of the loaf which her mother, who was looking in stubborn silence at the ground, still held in her hand. When she had finished, she stood up and began to clear the table and wash the dishes. Her mother did not speak. Sometime afterwards Pauline, without thinking, started singing as she worked. Alexander got down from his chair and went out to play.

Although Mr Nettle lived with these people and was continually called upon for sympathy by Mrs Clark, and although Pauline came under his notice pretty often, sometimes sulking or in a fury and sometimes smiling at him in the impertinent way that irritated him so much, and he might have thought at least that she was an interesting and curious personality, he could not be said to be interested in them at all. He did not have very much society, and he stayed at home much of the time alone, except that sometimes he went to his uncle's for supper. But there he sat quietly and only answered their inquiries and smiled at them without feeling in any way at home there, and they were used to thinking of him as very shy, and scarcely troubled about his inability to converse with them. But if ever he met any of the people from Olivia's house, then he was very happy to be with them and heard everything they said as though it were important and of significance in his own life, as if they were in a way beings from another world. And I do not think that this was entirely because Olivia's beauty had suddenly made so deep an impression on him, but that, added to this, they really were people whose life was in every way different from his, while Pauline and her mother and Alexander were quite ordinary things in his life, and were painted in the dull colours of everything that is too near.

It is amusing to think that George Curle who, with all his amiability, had moments when he was a little ridiculous, should also have been lighted up by this glory, but it is a fact that it was so to a certain extent. George Curle certainly now considered Nettle one of his friends, often sought him out and held long conversations with him, and so formed his chief link with Olivia and these people.

George Curle would very often be struck with some idea, and feeling the need to expound it to someone, and perhaps not finding anyone to listen to him sympathetically at home, he would go to call on Nettle and stay with him for part of the evening.

For example, one afternoon he was sitting with his mother; he had just put his book down to stroke the cat, and when he picked it up again he did not read, but keeping his finger in it to mark the place, began to talk.

"You know," he said, "living in the country suits me. I don't mean simply physically that I am well, though that also is very true, but spiritually."

"Nonsense," said Mrs Curle heavily, going on with her knitting in a dispirited manner.

"No, it is perfectly true," said George good-humouredly.

"There is nothing at all to amuse people in the country," said his mother.

"No, but all the same," said George, "there is something very good for the soul in seeing how the trees and things are quite content to go on doing the same thing year after year, having leaves and fruit and then losing them again. It makes one see," he continued, moving a cushion that he was half sitting on and arranging himself more comfortably in his chair, "not at all that ambition and human aspirations and that sort of thing are ridiculous, but that they should not be discouraged by a certain monotony in the results of their achievements. Don't you agree?"

"Nobody ever does anything here but talk," said Mrs Curle.

"So did the Greeks," said George triumphantly; "they always talked. That is really true, you know," he added anxiously, seeing that she had not been much affected by the instance.

"What was the good of it?" asked Mrs Curle.

"Oh, come now," said George, looking at her reproachfully and a little with annoyance, "you can't ask a question like that."

He kept looking at her for a few moments, but she was staring out through the window at the grey sky, and he opened his book and began reading again. But he had scarcely read a page when he resumed the discussion.

"I should not, you know, call myself a man entirely without ambition," he said musingly.

"I should hope not," said his mother in a half-complaining voice. "Your father was very ambitious, though it did not lead him anywhere in particular."

"But you see what I mean?" said George urgently. "After

all, when you think of Indian thought and philosophy, of the Oriental point of view in general, you can't help seeing ambitious people as simply rushing wildly to and fro all to no purpose. But what I said was, that trees and that sort of thing show you that ambition is not something ridiculous at all, but simply a kind of mystic humility which makes a man think with fear and joy of the very things that he, and he alone, is constructed to perform."

"Nonsense," said Mrs Curle. "That is not what you said, and you are simply mixing things up."

George went back to his book disconcerted, and remained disconcerted and even aggrieved for the rest of the afternoon, so that some time after tea he put on his hat and coat and went down the hill to call on his new friend Mr Nettle.

He sat down in an armchair before Nettle's fire and tried at once to bring the conversation round to the interesting subject which had occupied him before. Next to starting a conversation, the thing of which Nettle was most incapable was stopping one, so after a very short interval George Curle was saying –

"It seems to me that there is something rather of a mystic character about ambition; don't you agree?"

"I don't know quite what you mean," said Nettle looking down into the fire.

"Well," began Curle, smiling happily, with the platform to himself, and he was about to repeat his thesis of the afternoon when it occurred to him to ask, "Would you call yourself ambitious, for example?"

"I don't know," said Nettle.

"You see, I mean, for instance, would you like to play the cello perfectly or wouldn't you?"

"No, not that," said Nettle; "but of course there are a lot of things I should like to do, only each would make the other impossible."

"Yes, but what do you want most of all?" asked George

eagerly. "What would you call your greatest wish in the world?"

Nettle blushed a little, and put his head awkwardly on one side. He was for a moment silent.

"I should like to be quite well," he said afterwards.

"Are you ill, then?" asked George anxiously.

"Not now," said Nettle, "but I often get ill in the winter."

George Curle looked at him thoughtfully, but afterwards he said, "Well, what do you think – would you call yourself ambitious?"

"I don't know," said Nettle.

"Well, you know, strictly speaking, I don't think one would really call that ambition, if you don't object to my saying so." He looked at him for reassurance.

Nettle smiled.

"So that means," George resumed, "that ambition is, one might say, more limited. You know, that seems to me very extraordinary, that you should want to do things which you know are impossible. You see, I only want to do things which it seems to me that I shall be able to do."

Nettle smiled again shyly.

"Of course, what it all amounts to," said George suddenly, feeling a little disappointed in his theory, "is that the ambitious man has to feel bound by reality." He paused and looked into the fire as if seeking some of the ardour he had had for the idea.

"No," said Nettle suddenly, and with surprising decision, "not by reality, only by the material world."

"Oh," said George Curle in surprise, "do you really think so?"

They talked a bit longer about general things, but it must be quite clear from what has been reported of their conversation the advantages that they derived from this exchange of ideas. Soon afterwards George Curle went home.

Nettle sat looking into the fire for a long time, and then he got up and fetched some notepaper from the top drawer of the sideboard. He played with a pencil for a bit with his thin hands, and then with a shy smile and the same turn of his neck with which he accompanied anything that he remarked aloud, he wrote:

Thou art the fairest flower in the world.

He looked at it, even a little alarmed. Then since, as everyone knows who has tried to write poetry before, practically nothing rhymes with *world*, he crossed it out and wrote instead:

Thou art like the fairest flower in May.

He wanted to point out that she wore a garland of white flowers round her head, and then, after a description of the flowers, that while they have the effect of making him, the author of the poem, sad, her eyes, which are themselves rather sad, have quite the opposite effect because they seem to be kind and reassuring; but this was very difficult to put into lines and to rhyme. Before he went to bed he had added to it,

Which opens at the dawning of the day,

Which had rather taken him off the subject, since it was not really the flower that he was interested in.

A few days afterwards it began to rain. In the morning George Curle came down to the post-office in his mackintosh, and asked Nettle to come up that evening.

It rained all the afternoon, and though it had stopped by the evening the sky was quite dark and there was no moon. Nettle walked slowly up the hill. To-night when he reached the house the fir trees did not look very green; they were only black, and everything else melted off into the grey shadows. Suddenly, as he was standing outside the door in the darkness, he had a curious feeling of loneliness, as though he did not actually know the people he was going to visit. But when he had rung the bell the door opened and Olivia was there, smiling at him gently. She led him through the lighted hall into the drawing-room. Eleanor and Mrs Curle were there already, and after a moment George came in. He came to shake hands with Nettle, smiling with the utmost friendliness of which even he was capable. Olivia was smiling at him, too, with her rather sad eyes and, as he turned his head to look at her and there was a little silence, Eleanor raised her eyes from looking at the carpet and laughed across at him. Her deep blue eyes looked up at him from under her rather high forehead. He looked again at Olivia.

He felt a bit like someone who, walking in some well-known place, suddenly wanders into fairyland, which, as is well understood, always happens to the most unlikely individual. When afterwards they went in to supper, and Mrs Curle sat at the top of the table gazing with her stupid and rather complaining expression at nothing in particular, she had to Nettle a curious air of having been sitting like that for many years already; and this added to the strange and pleasant feeling. Only once did the enchantment tremble and grow a little thin, and that was when Mrs Curle inquired again about Pauline Clark, and if she could not sing for them; and Eleanor at once suggested that he should bring her up there one day with him. He felt suddenly angry at Pauline's intrusion into this quite different world, and did not answer Eleanor, who was looking up at him and smiling. But except for this, the strange feeling persisted all the evening until he went and the door closed and he was shut out again in the darkness.

It had occurred to him in the middle of supper that he might ask them to come to tea with him, and having dared to ask this, he had looked down at the tablecloth and waited, feeling very embarrassed, for an answer. Mrs Curle had looked at him dispassionately and said that "the young people could go." George had quite eagerly helped him to find a day, and Olivia had smiled and thanked him, though perhaps a little absent-mindedly.

After that it rained very heavily nearly every day until the short pale grass was sodden with rain, and often there were large, curiously-shaped pools on the low flat fields. There was water in every hollow on the roads, and with every movement of the wind the green trees in the churchyard sent down showers of drops on to the graves. Every night, when there was a moon at all, it had a yellowish ring around it, which meant more rain, and in the morning the rain was still beating down.

One the Saturday that Nettle was expecting his visitors it was a little finer; the rain came only in heavy showers, and in between the sun shone out of the cold white sky. Nettle waited all the afternoon in the utmost anxiety, and he was half afraid that they would not come. But Olivia and George Curle came. He helped Olivia to take off her mackintosh in the passage. Eleanor was not with them, and they said nothing to him about her, and did not, for instance, tell him that she was unable to come for some reason. It seemed to him a little strange, but he did not ask.

Olivia went into the room and sat down in his armchair before the fire. She smiled at him kindly, but then looked out of the window as though she expected him and George to talk together and had herself only come in to wait until they had said all they had to say to each other.

George was talking but Nettle did not for the moment listen to him. He felt that the afternoon was in danger of turning out differently from what he had planned. He looked down at Olivia. Her head was turned a little as he had noticed her first of all; her rather round face was pale, and her large dark eyes looked towards the window. She did not notice that he was looking at her. George, leaning forward on his high chair, was still talking. Nettle, who was not yet fully attending to what he was saying but did not like to interrupt him, touched his arm and motioned to him to sit in the other armchair. George with a wave of his hand put the suggestion aside, and went on with what he was saying. So Nettle settled himself down in the armchair and tried, always looking from time to time at Olivia, to pick up the thread of the remarks.

She looked now at the fire. It seemed to him that she must be very young. It was strange that he always saw her with a garland of white flowers around her head. He was very happy to have her sitting there in his chair, only she did not speak to him. She was extraordinarily beautiful. He remembered that Eleanor was usually considered more beautiful; and he remembered her laughing up at him, and he felt a slight sensation of anger as he thought that she had not come and they had not said anything about it.

Afterwards though, when they had had tea and the light was on and they were sitting again before the fire, he lit a match and stood shyly with the match alight between his fingers to light Olivia's cigarette. She looked up at him with her large dark eyes and kept looking at him until it was lighted. He threw the match into the fire. It had burnt his fingers, a bit, not much. He lit another for George. They did not stay very long. Olivia stood up to go, and George, although he was practically in the middle of saying something, went with her, because, the truth is, that he had promised beforehand not to stay too long.

All the evening Nettle sat in the chair he had sat in in the afternoon, not his usual one. He had a book open on his knees, but he read very little. He stopped every few minutes to look at the other chair and to see if he could recall vividly to his mind exactly how she had looked sitting there. He had lighted her cigarette, and she had looked up at him with her large eyes. She had not spoken to him much. It seemed to him that she often looked at him with a disappointed air, as if her large sad eyes were seeking somebody else. It was quite clear what it meant. When she met him the first time he had spoken to her perfectly naturally and she had perhaps remarked to herself that he would have something interesting to say. It must have been because she spoke of him at home that he was first asked up there – to play, too, of course, but that was as good a way as another of beginning an acquaintance. On the first occasion he had been perfectly calm and master of himself. She had turned to go and asked, looking over her shoulder, "Will it go at once?" And he had answered, perfectly naturally, "Yes, certainly, at once."

But now he was always too shy to talk to her. The things that he would have liked to say to her sounded different and distorted when he began to say them aloud, and he stopped at once and did not finish the sentence and even blushed. But that slightly abstracted, disappointed air of hers in a way struck fear into his heart. He felt that he ought to do something before it was too late; he felt that he must do something very decisive so that she could see that all the time, behind his shyness, his own will had been working, as it were, towards the goal in view. It occurred to him that he ought to call there once. He would not make any remarks about having left music there; he would simply call on them just as George Curle visited him, and he would leave his cello at home. She would see why he had come, and smile at him and talk to him. He felt that there was an urgent need for this act of decision; but when he thought actually of doing it he sat forward in his chair, his forehead wrinkled a little as he tried to keep the idea before his eyes, and he stirred with the poker what remained of the fire. He thought that he would leave the details of the resolution to be decided on another day, though he was in a way rather excited, but he was tired. It had rained all the week, and that is tiring, and to-day he had been anxious.

He woke up next morning feeling downcast. He would have dismissed from his mind the idea of calling at Olivia's house on his own account, but it now seemed to him in some way a weakness to go back on it, and this feeling made him suddenly force himself to make up his mind to call there that very evening. But he was oppressed with a feeling of uncertainty. He could see vividly Olivia's dark eyes looking up at him, only now in the cold daylight he could not be sure what it was they urged him to do.

He walked along the street to the post-office. Anybody meeting him could tell that he was worried; his forehead was wrinkled and he looked down at the pavement in a perplexed sort of way. And that evening he did start up the hill without his cello, not very early because, of course, he did not want to invite himself to supper. He felt very anxious. He stopped before he got to the door, and stood for a few moments in the shadow of the fir trees. He took off his hat and drew his handkerchief across his forehead. When he got to the door, and had rung the bell, he suddenly experienced a feeling of peace and calm which took away his mistrust and doubt of himself. He waited almost eagerly for the door to open.

George Curle came to meet him, and he was pleased to see him, though it is true that he was rather surprised. Olivia and Eleanor and Mrs Curle were sitting reading; and they were surprised too when George brought Nettle in. He looked rather excited and he was clutching a pair of gloves tightly in both hands, though he must have been quite unaware of it.

Eleanor looked across at Olivia interrogatively, as if she meant to ask if she had told him to come, but she smiled and shook hands with him politely. Mrs Curle looked at him a little astonished, but she was not very much affected, and put down her book and took up her knitting.

Olivia smiled at him too and made him sit down. He still kept the gloves firmly in his hands, but he sat down smiling at them all and asked in a comparatively loud voice, "Where is your cat?" and since this was the first quite independent remark he had ever made in that house, it almost gave the rather absurd impression that he had this evening come there especially to see the cat.

Mrs Curle looked down at the carpet beside her chair. "It is not here," she said. "Go and fetch it, George."

George went smiling out of the room.

"I hope you were not tired after yesterday," said Nettle, smiling now rather shyly again at Olivia.

She was a little puzzled. "No?" she said inquiringly.

"Oh," said Eleanor suddenly, "I was very sorry not to be able to come to tea with you as I promised; I had a most frightful headache. Did Olivia tell you?"

Nettle looked at Olivia in some uncertainty, but she did not say anything and only looked across at her sister; so addressing Mrs Curle he remarked, "All this rain makes people have headaches."

"Yes, but only in the country," sand Mrs Curle. "In town, people don't go about with headaches just because it is raining."

Nettle, who had meant this remark to be quite general, was surprised at the vigour with which she said this, and did not find anything to say to it. He smiled a little doubtfully but he did not answer.

George came in with the cat in his arms. He put it down near Nettle. Nettle, holding his gloves in one hand, stroked it with the other. It hurriedly rubbed itself against his chair, and then ran across the carpet to Mrs Curle.

Eleanor laughed, and Nettle looking up smiled at her happily. If George had put forward some idea Nettle would have discussed it with him to-night, but it did not happen to be one of his eloquent moments. It was a good thing that Nettle had come prepared to talk, because otherwise there would not have been much conversation. But naturally he did not talk all the time, and there were long silences. But whatever he said they gave their attention to, and usually some talk followed from it. For instance, he looked at Mrs Curle's knitting and said, "I like purple very much. I think it is my favourite colour. What is yours?" he said to everyone in general.

"Do you know, I don't think I have a favourite colour. I like one just as well as another," said George in surprise, because this peculiarity of his psychology interested him very much.

"Of course you have," said Eleanor; "everybody has. Mine is yellow."

"Oh, Eleanor, it can't be," said Olivia; "yellow doesn't suit you."

"Yes, but it can be my favourite colour all the same," she said.

"Why do you like purple?" asked George.

"I don't know," said Nettle, but he added almost immediately, "I like purple flowers very much. They look innocent and queenly at the same time. I think they are very beautiful."

He looked at Olivia. She was looking at him thoughtfully, and she half smiled. He looked at her, quite losing consciousness of where he was, and he even put the gloves in his pocket. She said, "I think I like purple too, but a greyish purple, without any red in it."

Eleanor yawned.

Nettle stayed a long time; he did not seem to notice that they looked tired. When he had gone at last, Eleanor said, "Whatever made him call to-night. I do hope he doesn't take to coming here often. Did you ask him, Olivia?"

"No," she said.

"There is no need at all to be afraid," said George, slightly offended. "He was probably walking past and called out of a sense of duty."

"But he really is rather extraordinary," said Eleanor, "and he seemed so excited about something."

"Perhaps he is ill," said George warningly. "He says he gets ill in the winter."

"He looks awfully delicate," said Olivia. "There is really something rather pathetic about him. I think he's very nice."

"Yes," said Eleanor laughing; "he was rather sweet about the purple flowers. But you can't say that he is very entertaining." She yawned, stretching her arms up behind her head.

Nettle as he walked down the hill was in a state of triumph bordering on ecstasy. He went along the road unencumbered by the cello. The great tall trees at the roadside stretched out to the sky; it was rather a nice night, not very cold. As he neared the public-house at the foot of the hill some men came out of it, and then the lights went out in the bar-room. He walked slowly for a moment or two, so as not to have to walk home with any of them with whom he might be acquainted. One of the men went unsteadily along, singing confidentially to himself. The others soon turned aside in another direction, but when Nettle came near his house this one was still in front of him. Suddenly a stone skipped along the ground. The singing stopped, and curses took its place; then it was resumed, and the man turned the corner. Some suppressed laughter came from the doorway of Nettle's lodgings. Pauline Clark was there talking to someone. She was leaning against the door laughing, and neither she nor the boy noticed him.

Not exactly liking to walk up to the door without announcing himself, but with a feeling of surprising irritation at them, he stood for a moment in indecision. Pauline was standing with her back against the door, and her head stretched back until it also touched it. The moonlight was shining on her face, and she was smiling down at the boy, whose back seemed to express a certain uncouth awkwardness mingled with disturbed curiosity. He was saying in a half-threatening voice, "What are you laughing at?"

Pauline grinned, and turning her head saw Nettle standing on the pavement, and she laughed now almost aloud. The boy looked round hastily, and retreating to the side stood leaning against the house. Nettle walked up to the door, and without saying anything, proceeded to unlock it. Pauline put her hand on his arm and her head up to whisper to him, "Don't shut the door. I won't be a minute."

He shook her hand away with an uncontrollable annoyance. He had become, for some reason, angry. Pauline shrugged her shoulders and made a grimace to inform her friend that he was in a temper.

Nettle entered the house, but of course he left the door unlatched and went in to his sitting-room. But evidently she did not dare afterwards to stay long outside, because before he went upstairs she had come in and the door was shut. He did not sleep at once. The evening seemed to have stretched itself out, out of all reason. It seemed very long since he had sat in Olivia's house and looked at her and talked. He tried to think of it quietly, but all the time at the back of his mind there was a feeling of anger, and when he tried to trace it to its source, for some reason he always remembered Pauline standing against the door grinning at the boy, and in spite of the foolishness of remaining angry about what did not concern him in the least, the anger lasted and spoiled his thoughts which he might have enjoyed in peace after the events of that evening.

The moonlight shone right into his room. He lay with his eyes closed trying to sleep. But the moonlight worried him, and he got out of bed and pulled down the blind. After that he soon fell asleep.

Outside everything lay absolutely quiet in the moonlight. The bare grey trees held their branches up to heaven in almost comic attitudes of supplication; the yews in the churchyard took on a curious dark silvery colour; the low, black feathery hedges enclosing the fields participated in the flat receptiveness that the moon gives to everything. The square tower of the church, with its dark shadows, had a rather top-heavy appearance and seemed to be trying to bend over to look down on the empty white road. After such a light night, day came quite imperceptibly; it was only a psychological change.

Nettle remembered half-way through the morning that it was the day on which he had to play at the church social, but it did not worry him as much as might have been expected. All day he seemed to be pre-occupied, and often rubbed the back of his hand across his forehead as though he had a bad headache. He had a half-tired, half-perplexed expression on his face.

In the evening he put on his best suit and went over to the church hall, not at the beginning of the evening, because he was to play later on. When he got to the porch he had to wait there because something was going on inside. He put his cello to lean against the side and stood sideways against the glass of the door, to see the platform. It was Pauline Clark who had got up to sing; she was standing smiling at the audience, waiting for the music to begin. Somebody at the back of the hall clapped loudly, and her smile became a grin. The music started, and she sang. She was not at all self-conscious. Her voice was sometimes rich and deep and even very beautiful, sometimes in other passages it got curiously thin and colourless. She received the applause at the end with the same half-grin, and went down from the platform and across the hall smiling at her acquaintances.

Nettle took up his cello and carried it to the platform. He was a bit nervous as he felt all the eyes of the people there staring at him, but when he was on the platform and had started playing, his headache and a sudden quite vivid recollection of how he had talked about purple flowers to Olivia, and how she had said that purple was her favourite colour, but a greyish purple with no red in it, completely absorbed his attention, and he played in quite a preoccupied manner. His head was throbbing painfully; it seemed to him far more distinct than the beat of the music.

When it was over, he walked again towards the door, and would have gone out at once, only he happened to notice Pauline, and he stood looking at her with an absorbed attention that was really, however, caused by his headache. She was sitting by herself on the end of a bench. On the bench behind her two boys sat whispering and looking at her, and of this she appeared fully conscious. One of them leaned forward and pushed a packet wrapped in exercise-book paper and tied up with string into her hand. She looked at him over her shoulder and then let the packet lie on her lap, as though she felt a certain amount of scorn for the offering. But afterwards she opened it and began to eat the sweets that were inside. Just as Nettle turned to go out she turned round and offered the paper to the boys for them to take one.

Nettle went home and sat for some time in his chair. He even put a wet handkerchief on his forehead. Then he went to bed. In spite of the throbbing of his head, he felt a certain almost physical sensation of happiness. It was this secure feeling that Olivia's sad expression had in some curious way a connection with him, though of course it might have been caused by a lot of other things too. That was to be understood. But that she saw so clearly what he was like, although when he spoke to people he was shy and blushed, seemed to him true. The first time they had met he had been perfectly natural, as he really was in himself, and then when she met him again and he had not known how to talk to her or to answer, she was rather disappointed. He felt disappointed in himself too; he did not feel now that he could be as calm and as much master of himself as when he met her first. He saw her looking at him with her rather round pale face and large dark eyes. He had a sensation almost of touching the purple flowers he had talked about.

Suddenly he saw, with extraordinary vividness, the little scene when Pauline sat on the bench eating the sweets out of the paper, with the boys whispering behind her. But he felt that it had nothing at all to do with the world in which he lived. He did not feel even a momentary irritation; he was not interested. It was even strange that he should remember so vividly what did not interest him in any way.

The next day his headache had practically gone. When he was in the post-office in the morning Olivia came in to send a telegram. He felt somehow very much surprised to see her, though it was quite a natural thing that she should come. She went to the table to write it out and left her gloves there. When she came to give it to him she scarcely smiled. She looked all the time at the wire as he counted the words as though it were very important. She said that the weather was rather tiring, and turned to go. It seemed to him astonishing that she had happened to come there that morning and was going again so soon almost without speaking to him. She was perhaps tired. She was particularly pale. He looked after her, and then to the table where she had written. The gloves were still there. He called her. She looked back over her shoulder a little abstractedly, and then saw them and smiled at him to thank him before she went out. But afterwards he had an inexplicable feeling of disappointment. He sent off the wire. It appeared that they were expecting a visitor.

Often now that winter had come, Nettle felt not exactly ill, but a kind of tiredness seized on all his limbs, so that he was glad in the evenings to sit in his chair before the fire and read or think. On Saturday afternoons and Sundays he always went for walks, unless it was raining too badly, because it was good for his health, even though he felt more like staying in. Quite often, of course, he went to supper at his uncle's, but he sat there with them scarcely speaking. He went there this evening. The organist at the church was there too. They talked about one thing and another, but he sat looking at the floor and thinking sometimes so deeply of other subjects that he was hardly conscious of what they were saying.

Once somebody addressed some remark to him and he did not answer. His aunt laughed and said, "He must be in love."

He looked up apologetically, and then when he realised what she had said he blushed. The two men laughed, but the subject was not continued, because they did not know whom to tease him about. His uncle used to look at him sometimes and shake his head as he noticed how delicate he looked.

If by some chance they said something about the Nerans he heard at once what they were saying, because their words then seemed to penetrate deep down to his own thoughts. It was usually of the uncle who was dead that they spoke. He died comparatively young; he was very clever, at least if he had read all the books that he had there must have been a lot in his head. But nothing came of it all, except that most of his books were given to a library. Perhaps if he had lived a little longer he might have written one himself.

"My nephew reads a lot," Nettle's uncle added to the end of this discourse.

"It's a good thing to read," said the organist, shaking his head wisely.

"Yes, but not too much," said his aunt, looking warningly at Nettle.

His uncle laughed.

He sat there in the warmth, and when it was time to go he wrapped a scarf round his neck so as not to catch cold on the way home.

The next morning he woke up conscious of having dreamed something a little out of the ordinary. He could remember nothing of the dream, but he awakened still rather under its spell, and while he dressed he tried to bring it to mind. But he found that the effort of doing so was making him lose its enchantment.

At breakfast, when he had ceased to think about it and only the pleasant emotion remained at the back of his mind, he suddenly recalled something. There had been in it a large shield, with arms of some kind on it in pale red through which the silver seemed to shine. The shield was very big, as high as a man. The place appeared to be a desert. But the important thing was, of course, the extraordinary emotional significance this shield had for him. He rested his head on one hand and with the other moved the marmalade spoon slowly backwards and forwards.

It was not very early, and he hurried out. Alexander and the little boy from the next house were sitting on the edge of the pavement, and it happened that as Nettle hurried past they both laughed very loudly, probably, as children very often do, at nothing at all. Nettle looked round at them shyly and with mistrust. The other little boy looked at Alexander, and again both of them laughed. It was quite evident that this was at a preconceived signal, were it only from the fact that Alexander, though he laughed very loudly, did it entirely without mirth and preserved all the time a serious expression on the rest of his face.

Nettle looked in uncertainty up at the windows of the house. Pauline was leaning out of one of them, looking up and down the road and shaking a duster. She smiled down at him. He felt irritated. He went along the road as quickly as he could before the children could begin laughing again.

During the morning the large shield about which he had dreamed flashed again into his mind. Before he had not been able to remember anything of the dream except this itself, but now he could see quite clearly a hand mailed in silver holding the great shield by the strap, which was twisted firmly around the wrist.

He walked slowly back to his lodgings at mid-day. It was cold, but the feeling of extreme tiredness which he had had before came again. When he had had dinner he sat for a short time without moving in his armchair. He scarcely thought, and the shield from his dream which persisted in his mind seemed to have retreated to some distance and to have lost some of its emotional depth.

In the afternoon, when he was back at work, as often as he could he put his arms on his table and let his head rest on them, for he began to have a headache again, not a very bad one, but a slight throbbing pain which, combined with his tiredness, made him feel extraordinarily depressed. Outside the post-office window the bare stiff twigs of a tree knocked together a little in the wind and sometimes even tapped against the glass. Through the stiff, numbed branches one could see the sky sometimes grey and sometimes a pale dull blue. The street was empty except for someone who came in to send a wire. Nettle sent it off, and then rested his head again on his arms.

The girl from the telephone touched him on the shoulder. "Do you feel ill?" she asked.

He looked up. "No," he said, and smiled rather awkwardly.

"Lord, I'm sick of this weather," she said, turning away and yawning with her arms above her head.

Nettle looked after her. He would have made some remark about the weather but she had gone to the window and stood looking out. She had a dark red blouse on.

"I've got a splitting headache," she said to nobody in particular.

Nettle returned to his thoughts. The afternoon seemed terribly long. Yesterday morning Olivia had come in to send a wire.

"I love her," he thought to himself, but he simply thought the words without attaching much meaning to them. When it was time to go and he stood putting on his coat and wrapping his scarf round his neck he was still thinking of her. His headache had not gone, so he did not put on his hat, but went out carrying it in his hand.

Outside it was almost a different world, because the sun was setting. The sky above the horizon where there were no clouds was red, and from behind a grey cloud lined with the purest gold the sun, a ball of orange fire, descended into this red field and spread a golden glow over it. The rest of the sky took on a pale transparency, and the shadow of a moon appeared in it high over the black feathery trees.

Nettle looked up, letting the light cold wind brush his forehead. He did not feel quite so tired. Suddenly the dream that he had had the night before came into his mind, all at once like a chord of music, so that he could not be certain which part of it came first. For it seemed that the hand mailed in silver held the great shield with its pale red device, through which the silver shone, against the rush of thousands of bright silver spears, and that he stood alone in the same place, which was a kind of desert, under a pale moon, looking on the ground, which was disturbed everywhere with the prints of horses' hoofs, at a garland of white flowers made to fit a woman's head. There was the loud metallic sound of a gong, and from the east there came something shining with red and gold like the procession of a king and that must have been the sun rising. It was in a way a very beautiful dream. Nettle walked slowly along with his hat in his hand looking at the pavement and thinking about it.

The clouds moved slowly across the sky. The moon was often scarcely visible against the pale grey, and sometimes it was lost altogether. It waited for the sun to disappear, but the sun still kept a riot of splendour in the sky. The soft clouds were bathed in pale reddish gold.

Upon the hill the white wall of the Nerans' house was pale pink in the dying light, except where the dark green branches of the little fir trees hid it. Olivia came out of the gate with a gentleman who had come that day to visit them. They walked together down the hill. Olivia looked up at the scarcely visible moon, and for some reason pointed it out to her companion. He looked around him with interest as he walked. He was rather short and exceedingly pale, though one side of his face was now bathed a little in the golden red glow of the sun.

They met Nettle in the village. He did not see them at first, because he was looking down at the pavement still thinking of his rather extraordinary dream, and Olivia had actually stopped in front of him and spoken to him before he looked up. He stopped and half smiled at her. His hat was already in his hand, and he stood holding it firmly, but he did not say anything. She introduced him to Mr David Premiss. It was the visitor they had been expecting, and Nettle remembered his name from the wire. He did not pay a great deal of attention to Nettle, but looked with interest at the houses and at the people who passed, and while he did this, both Nettle and Olivia took the opportunity to look at him, and she was still watching him rather intently when Nettle turned away to look once more at her. They were standing there on the pavement and yet not saying anything.

Nettle put his hand out to shake hands with her, although it was not altogether necessary when they had just met on the street. She shook hands with him and smiled and touched Mr Premiss's arm to bring him out of his absorption. He turned towards them, shook hands a little absentmindedly with Nettle, and they walked on. Nettle looked after them for a moment, as it were, a little confused between his dream and the sudden appearance of these two people. As he stood there Mr Premiss turned round, evidently because Olivia was saying something about him, and seeing that he too was looking back, he smiled and waved his hand in the most friendly manner possible.

Nettle walked on. There was a thin line of grey cloud across the middle of the sun, which was already near the horizon, but soon it drifted away. Some of the windows in the village reflected the red light. The sun hovered for a moment on the horizon and then went slowly down behind the dark hill. Except for a cloud right above it whose edges reflected all the orange splendour of the invisible sun, the colours in the sky became paler, the palest red and the palest gold, merging at last into the grey of the eastern sky. A few stars had come out. It began to grow dark in the village, and soon in the sky there was left only a patch of brightness where the sun had long disappeared. When that too was gone, the moon and the few stars seemed to be shining with a bright silver light over the cold grey earth.

CHAPTER 2

Mr David Premiss, going out into the garden on the morning after his arrival and finding Eleanor there, was more struck than he had been the day before with her beauty. It is true that his friend George Curle had spoken very often about both his cousins with enthusiasm, and had particularly mentioned this fact, but, though he had a sincere affection for George and always listened to him with attention, even when he was amused at him, he did not very much trust his judgment, particularly of women. He looked at Eleanor, very carefully hiding his appreciation. She looked up at him with her blue eyes and smiled.

She looked at him with admiration, because she had heard a lot about him from George, and she had also read a volume of essays by him which she had not fully understood. She hoped that, when he had finished regarding the scenery, he would speak to her again, perhaps of something of the utmost importance, and she was awfully surprised when, after giving his attention to the bare garden and the little fir trees and the curving line of the hills and the cloudy masses of leafless trees here and there in the distance, he turned and went in without saying anything at all.

Later in the day he went for a walk by himself, and though he was not very fond of the country and scarcely ever visited it, he was struck and rather charmed by the subdued colours and delicate lines of the season. It seemed to him that the little trees with their feathery black branches and the soft grey sky had an air of restrained gaiety like a little scherzo in a minor key.

On this enchanting and subtle effect of winter he remarked to Olivia when he returned to the house. She smiled at him with her large eyes, and afterwards, when he sat down with a book and began to read, she stood at the window with her back towards it and looked at him with attention.

Mr Premiss read with absorption, occasionally making some marks with a pencil on the margin of the book. Olivia would not have ventured to interrupt him, but, when once he moved his knees to let the book rest more securely on them while he wrote something at the side, he looked up, and seeing her looking at him, smiled.

Before he went back to the book, she said, "I am afraid that you will find it perhaps too quiet here for you, Mr Premiss. You know, there is no one interesting to talk to."

"Well now, suppose," said Mr Premiss, looking up politely but keeping his finger on the exact place in the book that he wished to note, "that I exhaust all the possibilities of conversation with everybody in this house, I am quite certain that there are other people somewhere near, because I have seen many houses and other signs of habitation."

She smiled uncertainly. "But there is scarcely anyone interesting," she said.

He had turned back to his book and was beginning to be lost in it again, but a few moments afterwards he looked up as it something else had struck him, and said, "Have you and your sister always lived here?"

"Yes," she said, "since the time when we were babies. We lived with our uncle, but he died last year." She looked down at the carpet.

He looked at her and said, "I had heard a great deal from George about his beautiful cousins."

She raised her eyes quickly and a little shyly and smiled. "George is our very good friend, you know," she said.

"He does not need to be, to say that," said Mr Premiss, interlacing the leaves of the book with his fingers, as if he were going on reading. Olivia looked at his book and at him anxiously, feeling she ought perhaps not to talk any more and interrupt him, and she did not answer.

But George did not have quite this respect and awe for Mr Premiss's time, and above all he was eager to take him, for some reason, to see Mr Nettle. Eleanor was shocked at the idea.

"But he will bore you to death," she said. "He never speaks a word."

"Eleanor!" said Olivia, "that is very unkind of you."

"But I can't help saying what is true," said Eleanor.

"It isn't true at all," said George impatiently. "It is only when you are always laughing at him that he is too shy to talk."

Eleanor laughed at this obvious prevarication.

Mr Premiss looked at her and suddenly smiled. "You are young, Miss Eleanor, and you do not realise how important it is for one to meet stupid people."

"Oh, but he isn't stupid," said Olivia.

"No, of course he isn't," said George irritably, frowning at Eleanor.

She looked at Mr Premiss. "Will you risk it?" she said.

"I will go with pleasure," he said gravely and politely.

In the evening he and George actually went to call on Nettle. He was pleased to see them, but rather surprised. He himself sat on a high chair, so that they should have the arm-chairs. He wondered very much who Mr Premiss was, because he seemed to him to have an air of distinction.

George Curle sat back in his chair with a grave expression on his face as though he had come there especially to ask something of the greatest importance and not merely to make his two friends acquainted. He had as a matter of fact a sudden suspicion that perhaps he would not succeed in putting them enough into contact with each other to make Premiss see the originality and interest of Nettle's character as he himself saw it, and he was wondering what subject it would be best to introduce. Premiss did not help him because, instead of speaking, he sat still in his chair, and with an air of the greatest politeness avoided examining Mr Nettle or anything in the room, and had turned his eyes inwards upon himself. And this sort of thing really continued during the whole visit, so that George began to feel something of the same disappointment that Eleanor and Olivia had felt at their first encounters with him. He felt in a sort of way that these two were two distinct sides of himself, and it was a source of disappointment and annoyance to him that two portions of his personality should sit on either side of the fire-place and fail to drop into conversation. It was not of course that they sat in silence, for besides George's fruitless attempts to launch them into deeper waters, Premiss quite often, looking at Nettle with what appeared to be a sudden interest, would ask some question or other.

He said, "Have you lived here long?"

"No," said Nettle. "I came here this winter so as not to spend the winter in town."

"Do you like living here?" he asked again.

"Yes," said Nettle, smiling a little.

"You like the country?"

"Yes," said Nettle again.

Premiss smiled, not at him but at the fire, and seeing that George, who could not see the use of small-talk, had on his face an expression of irritation and impatience, he laughed.

But towards the end of the evening something happened which made Mr Premiss lose his air of polite inattention, and from that moment he became exceedingly amiable and even gay. For just as they were getting up to go, Pauline Clark's light tap came at the window and Nettle looked around him uneasily.

"What was that?" Premiss asked, because he was rather nervous.

Nettle for some reason blushed a little. "It is my landlady's daughter. She comes in this way sometimes so that her mother shan't know how late she stays out."

Premiss laughed and followed him to the window. Nettle pulled up the blind and Pauline was there, standing outside with her hand on the pane. She looked in surprise at Mr Premiss, and he, while Nettle was turning away to go and open the door, lifted the window and put out his hand to help her in that way. She smiled and climbed in, and then stood in the room looking at the two men and at Nettle standing by the door. She did not know who Mr Premiss was, but she looked at him with interest, not disturbed by the fact that he was looking at her. He had small, very elegant shoes of soft leather, and he was very carefully dressed and had a ring on the little finger of his small white hand. She noted with surprise that he had a white handkerchief, not a coloured silk one which had hitherto appeared to her the unmistakable sign of smartness. When she at last looked up he was laughing at her as though he knew for certain what she was thinking. She bit her lip and her smile gradually changed into a grin.

Nettle came and shut the window behind her.

"Have you been for a walk?" asked George Curle politely.

She looked at him. "Yes," she said shortly and with suspicion.

She watched Mr Premiss take up his gloves from the sideboard and say good-night to Nettle. He held the door for her to go out before him into the passage. She went slowly up the stairs looking down at them over her shoulder, and as Mr Premiss went out he took off his hat and made her a low bow from the pavement, laughing all the time with immense amusement.

She ran into her room and to the window and knelt on a box in front of it to watch him going along the road in the moonlight. He was shorter than George Curle and he had put his arm through his and was walking along talking very seriously and intently. She pressed her face against the window so as to see them as long as possible.

A few mornings afterwards, quite early, when she was in Mr Nettle's room, she saw Mr Premiss pass the house as if he were going for a walk, for it was a fine though cold morning. She ran out into the passage and, pulling her coat hurriedly on over her working dress and pinafore, she slipped out of the house. She ran down a road which would lead her back to the main road, along which he was walking, without her having to pass him. She ran very quickly until she was quite warm. When she came to the main road again she stopped. Her heart was beating quickly, partly from the running and partly from her anxiety not to miss him. She looked up and along the road. He was just turning the corner and coming towards her. Her heart gave two big thumps. She was still out of breath, but she began to walk on, as if she too were going for a walk, but so slowly that he would catch up with her in a very short time. She did not look round until he was right behind her. He would have passed on the other side of the road without noticing her, but she looked round at him and smiled, and he recognised her.

"Hullo! Good morning," he said smiling.

She smiled again for answer.

"Are you going for a walk?" he asked.

She did not think it necessary to answer, but smiled again, as she hurried to keep up with him, for he walked rather quickly.

"This is rather a nice place, you know," he said. "Do you like living here?"

"It's all right," said Pauline.

He looked at her reflectively.

"Perhaps you would prefer town life. What do you think?"

"I don't know," she said.

He regarded her with a certain amount of curiosity, but walked on without speaking. Pauline with her enviable faculty of being able to forget everything but the minute which occupied her, thought of nothing and only looked at

him as he walked on a little in front of her. But he was interested to see how the black branches of the trees looked like
little feathers, or like charming black lace through which the
delicate grey morning sky showed with an almost transparent
softness, and of what a deep green were the branches of the
firs against this grey. It was a fine morning, and here and
there the grey shaded off almost imperceptibly into the palest
blue.

When he turned to go back Pauline turned too.

"You don't go any farther?" he asked.

"No," she said.

He did not conceal his amusement. "You like a walk
exactly the length that I like it?"

She smiled, not knowing precisely why he was so much
amused, and then becoming serious again resumed her intent
watching and her walk by his side.

He had not slept well, and he was a little tired. He looked
down at the road as he went and began, forgetting about the
girl, to think of the work he intended to do that morning.

"Have you come to live here?" asked Pauline suddenly.

He looked round at her in surprise, because he had already
become so absorbed in what he was thinking about, and said,
"No, I have come for a holiday."

"For how long?" she asked.

He laughed, but then answered, "For a few weeks only;
until after Christmas perhaps." He laughed again, very much
amused at her curiosity.

"Do you know Mr Curle?" he asked.

"The fat gentleman who comes to our house to see Mr
Nettle?" she asked.

"Yes," he said, and noticing her lack of enthusiasm, he
asked, "Don't you like him?"

She tossed her head a little. "I don't know," she said; "he's
rather funny."

"You are evidently without discrimination," said Premiss

and nodded at her impressively, though still with amusement, to confirm the statement.

Pauline smiled at him suspiciously, not at all understanding what he meant, but since it was evident that he was only laughing she was not perturbed but walked serenely on without answering. She had on a loose greyish-green coat of some rough material; she was rather short and thickset; she wore no hat, and her rather untidy short hair of no distinctive colour was caught insecurely into a slide at the back of her head so that some of it blew about in the wind.

When they reached the place where she had met him she stopped reluctantly.

"You go that way?" he asked.

She nodded.

"Good-bye," he said, and waved his hand as he walked away through the village, leaving her to hurry down the other road. He went gaily along. He saw Mr Nettle walking on the other side of the street to the post-office. He remembered him and shouted "Good morning" across to him; and when Nettle, who had not seen him, looked up to see who was being spoken to, he greeted him with a friendly gesture and walked on. He met a small girl on the pavement; she had a torn red frock and curls. Premiss, who was very fond of children, stopped at once and said to her, "Where are you going?"

She put her finger in her mouth and looked up at him, evidently a little put out at being addressed by a stranger.

"Shall I have a curl?" he asked.

She shook her head, and even took her finger out of her mouth and said "No." He went on, but he looked back and saw that she was looking after him with serious eyes, her finger in her mouth again. "Another conquest," thought Premiss, smiling to himself. He went up the hill between the tall trees where the old nests of the rooks still hung, and up to the house.

When it happened that some days afterwards Mr Nettle was asked up to play for them and somebody again suggested that Pauline Clark should come up to sing, not only Eleanor, who had approved of this project from the beginning, was enthusiastic over the idea, but Premiss took it up with such eagerness that Nettle found himself promising to convey the request to her and to bring her up on the evening which they fixed, though he had no desire at all to do so, and if he had not felt rather helpless in Premiss's hands he would have defended himself from the subject in evasive silences. He disliked very much even having to give Pauline the message.

She came into his room to clear away the tea-things, and he said, "Miss Neran would like you to go up there and sing a song for them."

"Which Miss Neran?" she asked.

"All of them up at the house," he said, a little impatiently.

She half smiled. "When?" she asked.

"You are to go up there Thursday evening, about seven o'clock. Take something with you to sing. You are not to stay there long, you know," he added in explanation, "but just to sing a song or two, and then go home."

Pauline considered this in silence. She was perfectly satisfied with the idea, and did not take his advice at all in bad part.

"Will that visitor be there?" she asked.

"Mr Premiss," said Nettle. "His name is Mr Premiss."

She gathered the tea-things together and reflected for a moment with some satisfaction. "Seven o'clock?" she asked as she went out of the room.

Mr Nettle nodded rather irritably.

The next evening she put on her dress that she wore on Sundays. She wanted to put on the white dress that she had worn for confirmation and on flower-Sundays, but her mother would not let her, and it was getting a bit small for her. She started up the hill by herself.

If it had been Mr Premiss or George Curle who had been asked to bring her up there, they would have walked up with her quite naturally, but Mr Nettle, since he could not stay away altogether, deliberately waited for half an hour after she had gone before he started. When he got to the house he could hear her singing. As he thought that she really had a beautiful voice, he quite saw that it was very reasonable that they should want her there to sing to them.

He went into the drawing-room just as she had finished her song. She was smiling, and Mr Premiss had walked up to the piano and was clapping his hands softly together and saying, "Encore, encore!" He looked up at Nettle without smiling, and began to look through the rather torn and dirty volume of Pauline's songs with Olivia.

"Who teaches you these songs?" he asked over his shoulder.

"The organist," she said, still standing up smiling serenely, and prepared to sing again.

"Can you sing any of the Bach?" he asked.

She looked at him blankly, because she did not know the names of the composers.

"Look, this one," he said, going up to show her.

She smiled and nodded her head.

He took the book back to Olivia and went to his chair. Pauline sang again. Afterwards, looking at Mr Nettle, bending down from his chair to take the cover off his cello, she remembered what he had said, and instead of standing ready to sing another song, she edged a little towards the door, though she was still smiling, and she did not say anything, and was very reluctant to go.

"Where are you going to?" asked Mr Premiss looking at her in surprise.

She grinned, because she hoped that he would not let her go yet.

"Aren't you going to sing again? Don't you know any more songs?" he asked.

"Yes," she said, rather relieved.

"Sit down here," said Mrs Curle, pointing to a chair near her.

Pauline made a sort of grimace at Mr Premiss which amused him very much, and then she went to sit down. Eleanor sat looking at her all the time.

Nettle began to play. He did not play very well, because he felt rather angry, though by this time he was not sure why. He did not somehow feel as happy there as he used to. After he had played, though, and the others were talking, Olivia smiled across at him from the piano and said, so that he heard it but the others did not, "Will you play again?" and he shook his head and frowned a little to show her that he did not want her to ask it aloud. She smiled and looked down at the keys, and he looked at her for a minute, not listening to what the others were saying.

Pauline sat on the chair looking up at Mr Premiss, who was laughing at something that George had said.

"Will you sing again?" said Eleanor, smiling at her a little shyly.

Pauline did not hear her, and did not answer.

"Sing," said Mrs Curle.

Pauline looked round at her.

"Are you going to sing?" Mrs Curle repeated, quite severely.

"I don't mind," said Pauline, and stood up. She sang two more songs. She knew then that it was time for her to go. She did not sit down but stood waiting for an opportunity to announce her departure.

"Are you going?" asked Eleanor.

"Yes," said Pauline.

Eleanor got up to come with her, and called George. Pauline walked slowly out of the room, looking over her shoulder at Mr Premiss, who was speaking to Olivia at the piano so intently that he had not noticed her. Olivia saw that she was going.

"But here is your music," she said, and gave it to George to carry out for her.

Mr Premiss looked up and smiled and waved his hand, and she followed Eleanor out. Eleanor took down her coat and helped her on with it.

"Haven't you a hat?" she asked.

"No," said Pauline.

"Don't you ever wear one?"

"Only on Sundays."

"You are not afraid to go down the hill in the dark?" asked George. "Mr Nettle is not coming yet."

"No," said Pauline rather scornfully.

George was relieved, because he did not want to have to accompany her.

"George," said Eleanor mysteriously.

He took out of his pocket a box of chocolates, tied with yellow ribbon, and gave it to Pauline.

She looked at him in surprise.

"Is it for me?" she asked.

George nodded benevolently.

"Yes, of course," said Eleanor. "It is because you have sung so nicely."

Pauline smiled and put it under her arm. Eleanor went to the door with her and watched her going down the path. She clutched the box of chocolates tightly. She was feeling rather excited; she would have liked to look inside the box, but it was dark under the trees. Before she got to her house she hid it under her coat, holding it in place with her arm. When she got in she did not tell her mother much. Mrs Clark was sitting by the kitchen fire waiting for her. She looked up at her suspiciously, from habit, although it was early and she knew where she had been. Pauline smiled.

"Did you sing?" asked Mrs Clark.

"Yes," said Pauline.

"What did they say?"

"They said it was nice."

"Who was there?" she asked gain, while Pauline stood with her back to the door, taking care not to let the chocolates fall to the ground.

"Only both Miss Nerans and their aunt and the fat gentleman," said she indifferently; "and Mr Nettle," she added as an afterthought.

"All right, go and get your coat off," said her mother.

Pauline hurried to the passage to hang up her coat, and ran quietly upstairs in the dark to hide the chocolates in a drawer in her bedroom.

"What did you want to go upstairs and wake your brother for?" said her mother.

"I didn't wake him," said Pauline. She sat down at the table and began to eat her supper. She was hungry. She felt happy. When she had finished she washed up the dishes and tidied up without being told to.

"Can I go to bed now?" she asked.

"Yes," said Mrs Clark, looking at her searchingly.

Pauline went upstairs, and undressing in the dark got quietly into bed. She lay with her eyes open until she heard her mother go to bed, and then, lighting the candle, she went to the drawer to see what the chocolates looked like and if there were two layers. She removed all the paper from the top and looked at them. They were arranged in the form of a star and wrapped in different coloured papers. And there *was* a layer underneath. She would have gone back to bed, but she felt the need of talking about the evening and showing someone the chocolates, so she woke Alexander with as little noise as possible, and, cautioning him to be quiet, she held open the box on the bed for him to see. He looked up at her with wide-open sleepy eyes and then down at the beautiful star.

"Where'd you get it?" he whispered.

"Up at the Nerans," she said. "I've been there to sing; and then the gentlemen gave me this."

"What gentlemen?" said Alexander, smoothing the top of the silver chocolate with his finger.

"You know the fat gentleman who lives there, the one who comes to see Mr Nettle?"

Alexander nodded solemnly.

"Well, him," she said, "and another much nicer gentleman, who is a visitor."

"Which one gave it to you?" he asked.

"Well the fat one *handed* it to me," she said, "but it was from both of them. There's another layer underneath."

Alexander in awe poked his finger down at one corner to feel.

"Look," she said, and carefully lifted the dividing cardboard so that he could see as well as feel. Then she took three of them out and gave two to him and took one herself. He received them in surprise, but when she took the box away and closed it he whispered, "Let me see it again."

"I'll keep the silver paper for you when I've eaten them," she said kindly, opening it. And then in a sudden supreme impulse of generosity she said, "You can take one from the top, whichever you like."

It was difficult to choose. He chose one wrapped in shining pinkish-red paper. And then she put the box back in the drawer and blew out the candle. Soon afterwards she fell asleep, even before Alexander had finished his third chocolate.

Mr Premiss unfortunately suffered very badly from sleeplessness, and spent many nights quite unable to sleep except for an hour or two in the early morning. And though the short sleep into which he fell was very deep, he awoke from it suddenly and passed directly into such complete wakefulness that he did not find it tolerable to remain longer in bed. It was for this reason, since breakfast was only at nine o'clock, that he so often went for a walk in the morning.

After coming up the stairs, talking and laughing with his

friends, he would bow theatrically to Olivia and Eleanor, perhaps suggest a romantic theme for George's dreams as he opened the door of his room, and then, once inside, he was faced by the necessity, and even the slight dread, of trying to sleep. For no sooner was the light out and he lying on his bed, than he became more concentratedly awake than ever during the day and in a way that would not have been actually unpleasant, had he not felt anxious about the exhaustion which would most certainly follow this continued sleeplessness. He did not toss from side to side on his pillow, but lay perfectly still on the wide bed with his small hands spread out on the sheet, until towards morning his anxiety, rather than any physical discomfort, made him get up and devise some means of persuading himself to sleep; so that often the morning light, coming into the room, would find him wrapped in his dressing-gown sleeping almost upright in a chair except that his head would have fallen to rest against the back and there would be a rather strained expression on his pale face, as if it were through some effort of his own that he kept himself asleep so long. Or sometimes he would be lying in what looked like a very uncomfortable position on the sofa, one hand and the girdle of his dressing-gown touching the floor.

After one night like this, he wakened suddenly, and when he had dressed, went out and walked down the hill in the cold morning light. The sun had just risen and had left a pale gold glow in one half of the dull white sky. There was a thin frost on the ground, enough to make the hard road glisten here and there, whenever the light of the sun penetrated a little more strongly through the clouds. Mr Premiss turned into a field where he sometimes walked. The grass was almost white with the frost, and even from a distance the hedges looked silver instead of black. At the end of the field the grass was longer and the silvered branches of some bushes grew out of it. Mr Premiss stood still for a moment and looked around him and at the dull sky from which the golden glow had now all disappeared.

Pauline Clark in her loose, thick, greenish-grey coat came walking through the field towards him. He laughed as she came up to him, and stamped his feet lightly on the ground to keep them warm as he waited for her.

"Why do you get up so early?" he asked, still laughing.

"My mother makes me," she said.

"And why do you come out for a walk before breakfast, just when I do?"

She smiled, not knowing exactly what to say.

"It is very good for one's health," said he seriously, beginning to walk on, but looking straight into her eyes and laughing again. She smiled back at him. They walked on together to the end of the field and into a wide lane. Premiss looked down at his small shoes and began to take care to walk in the middle of the path so that they should not get wet from the grass. She went on a little in front of him, and he looked with interest at the short, rather thick-set figure in the coarse thick coat. He put his gloved hand out and pulled a strand of her hair loose from her coat collar. It was not very pretty hair.

"Won't your hair grow any longer or do you cut it short?" he asked.

"No, it isn't cut. It's always been like this. It won't grow."

"But you ought to brush it," he said with interest. "Sit like a mermaid on your bed and brush it for an hour every night. Yes, really. You don't believe me, but that is how mermaids get their lovely golden hair."

He began to push the hair back inside her collar, and, since she showed no reluctance, laughing with immense amusement, he kissed her once or twice. He stood looking at her to see what effect it had produced, but she was looking at him equally attentively to see if he was going to kiss her again.

He laughed, and opened the gate for them to regain the road, and there they separated, for him to go up the hill and for her to go home. He stood watching her hurrying away, and when she turned, he waved his hand in his fur-lined glove.

He spent the morning reading, and in the afternoon he would have gone on reading too – he never attempted to sleep in the daytime, – but though he held the book in his hand his mind wandered with amusement to the morning's meeting with Pauline Clark. Mrs Curle and George were sleeping and Olivia was not at home. Sometime afterwards, Eleanor came into the room and found him asleep in his chair. It was a cold day and she had wrapped round her a white shawl of Olivia's. She stirred the fire as quietly as she could, and then sat down and studied Mr Premiss attentively. She admired him very much. She knew that he was very clever. Now, with his head resting sideways on his hand, and his eyes closed, he looked very young. She wondered if he was in love with anyone, and it occurred to her suddenly that he never seemed to write to anyone.

At this moment he moved a little and sighed. She thought that perhaps he was cold, for when she came into the room the fire was nearly out. She was going quietly to fetch a coat to put over him, but then she took off her shawl instead, and when she had put it lightly over him, she sat down on a foot-stool close to the fire.

He opened his eyes and, already feeling something over his hands, he looked down at the shawl, and then saw Eleanor's blue eyes regarding him with alarm.

"I am so sorry I woke you up," she said. "I put it so that you should not be cold."

"You were kindness itself," he said, standing up and picking up the shawl. She thought for a moment that he was angry, but he said, "Why, how heavy it is! Let me see if I can hold it on one finger." He held it for a moment hanging on his little finger, and then took it to her.

"Do you know what I dreamed?" he said, standing before her.

She shook her head.

"That someone shook an almond tree and the blossoms fell all over me."

"Did you really?" she asked in surprise, looking up at him, and holding up her hand for the shawl.

"No, let me put it on for you," he said, placing it on her shoulders, and kneeling down to arrange it carefully round her neck like a cloak.

"Did you really dream that it was almond blossoms?" she asked, because that seemed to her really interesting, though she blushed a little because he was kneeling on the carpet before her. Instead of answering, he laughed and got to his feet.

She was a little disconcerted, but she looked up at him with puzzled blue eyes.

"Now she is angry with me," he said in a tragic voice, turning to go back to his chair, and looking with absorption for his book.

"No, I am not angry," she said, "but I thought that it would have been so interesting if it were true."

"Did you see my book?" he asked, looking among the cushions of the chair and on the floor. He found it, and turned to her again.

"Very few things in this world are interesting," he said, and he had for the moment an expression of boredom and weariness on his pale face, but it changed almost immediately, and he looked straight at her and said with a laugh, "But there are many beautiful things. For example, you are extraordinarily beautiful. Do you know that?"

She looked at him reproachfully.

"No, really," he said with an air of great seriousness. "I simply say what you must know yourself. I don't flatter you. You have never heard me flattering anyone, have you?"

Eleanor reflected a moment, and was compelled to say that that was quite true.

"It must be nice to be a beautiful woman," he said, wrinkling his forehead and looking at the carpet, so that she did not know if he were thinking of what he was saying or of something else.

"Why?" she asked.

"Just to be beautiful for your own sake, without any thought of anyone else. I don't mean so that everyone shall fall in love with you, and princes and dukes fight for you – that, of course, will come, Miss Eleanor, – but simply to be beautiful, like a flower. That must be very nice. Isn't it?"

"I don't know," she said. "Of course I don't know at all," and she blushed a little and laughed up at him.

"Ah! how unhappy I am, when I think of the bad opinion you have of me!" he said suddenly, shaking his head and sitting down with his book.

"But, Mr Premiss, you know I think you are very clever."

"She thinks I am very clever!" said he mournfully, opening his book and beginning to read.

"But, Mr Premiss –" Eleanor began.

He made a comic gesture of despair, because he did not want to talk any more, and became at once completely absorbed in the book, so that, though she felt a little vexed at his sudden loss of interest, she did not dare to interrupt him. After a few minutes, however, she sat looking into the fire, equally absorbed in thinking of what he had said to her.

Mr Premiss worked all the afternoon and in the evening, until George Curle took him down to the station to meet Olivia, who had been away all day on a visit. He felt a bit tired. It was a rather nice night, frosty, but with a soft clear sky, full of stars. When they were waiting for the train he walked up and down to keep warm, lightly stamping his feet, and talking loudly to George, for there was no one on the platform. When Olivia came they walked back together.

"How cold it is," she said.

"Then you must do up your coat properly," said Premiss, and, making her stop, he very carefully buttoned it for her. She held her head up and looked at the stars as he fastened the collar.

"Walk on the other side of her," he said to George, "she is freezing."

"No, I am not quite freezing," she said laughing.

George pulled her hand through his arm and they walked on. Suddenly Mr Premiss came very close to her, pushed his arm through hers, and taking her hand squeezed it very hard so that it even hurt her a little. She looked at him; he was looking in front of him with a little smile on his face. The smile seemed to her rather self-satisfied, and the truth is that Premiss was rather accustomed to feminine admiration and was a little spoilt. His grasp relaxed, though he did not let her hand go.

"You know," said George, looking up at the sky and screwing up his eyes, "I don't really get any very definite feeling about stars. That sensation, that people say they get from a starry sky, of this being only one among millions of worlds, and they, in the face of this multitude, creatures of no significance whatever, I can't say I have ever really felt that at all. A starry night does not really make a great deal of impression on me."

"Oh," said Olivia, looking up again, "but look how beautiful they are!"

She moved her arm a little away, as if she wanted to pull her glove on more securely. Premiss did not seem to notice it, though he was looking at her quietly and he kept his arm lightly in hers, and said to George, "And look how beautiful *she* is!"

George lowered his gaze with interest and surprise.

Olivia looked quickly at Mr Premiss, but he met her eyes quite seriously and said, "No, really, those are the beautiful things in the universe, a beautiful woman, and children. You see, Miss Olivia," he continued, "there is in both of them a kind of natural aptitude for goodness; and after all, it is goodness that is the real secret of life."

"You mean goodness in a rather wide sense," remarked George hurriedly, anxious to be clear on this point.

"I mean it, whatever it turns out to be," said Premiss, laughing and looking at Olivia with amusement.

She smiled.

"No, really," he said, becoming serious again. "Why is it that I, a man really devoted to the most important things in life – I don't mean to be conceited, or to say that I achieve anything, but I can say that I am interested only in what one might call the 'higher things,' can't I?"

She nodded.

"Why then is it," he continued, "that I cannot order my life according to a consistent moral theory? Why is it that I cannot be master of my own life? Now, in children and in beautiful women one sometimes seems really on the point of grasping that secret. They seem to hold the enigma of the universe in their little hands."

He now seemed to be very much in earnest. George listened to him lost in attention. Olivia turned her head and regarded him a little shyly. They were at the gate, and he opened it in silence, thinking deeply as he held it open for Olivia to pass in. She looked at him; he was standing with his head bent as if he were looking on the ground, but he was quite absorbed in his own thoughts.

Eleanor met them as they went into the house; she put her arm round Olivia's waist, and they went upstairs together, talking about the friends she had visited.

It was late; Mrs Curle was already in bed. George went into the dining-room and came out eating a piece of cake. Premiss began to laugh.

"Look at him!" he said.

George smiled, and they went up the stairs. Outside his door Premiss paused a moment as if he would have liked to talk to George a bit longer, but then he opened the door and went in. The bed looked cold and uninviting. He went to the window and looked out for a few moments. The sky was beginning to be cloudy. Then he turned back and began to undress. He sat on the sofa, with this head resting on his hands and his forehead wrinkled. It would have been pleasanter to read, but he had been reading all day. It occurred to him not to go to bed at all, but to lie all night on the sofa. He took the eiderdown from the bed and put the light out, and he did in fact sleep excellently all night.

The next morning, when he looked out of his window, there was snow on the ground and a light powder of it on the trees. He decided, of course, not to go for his morning walk. All day the fields were white with their thin coating of snow, the branches of the fir trees bent a little under its weight, but what was most beautiful was that everywhere small trees, which had before stood like grey skeletons holding out their stiff cold limbs in despairing supplication to the hidden sun, now glistened with the snow and looked as though their bare grey branches had put forth blossoms by some magic. For a moment one could believe that one was passing by an orchard in the month when the trees are in flower, although it was cold and the sky was grey.

But very soon, even before night, the snow melted and only the grey bare branches were left dripping with the melted snow, and it seemed as if some lovely little princesses had turned into ugly bent witches. For winter is like the false Florimell, and her beauty melts away if it is touched.

The next day was grey and cold. They stayed in the house all day, talking and reading, but in the afternoon Mrs Curle, going out of the gate, found Pauline Clark walking slowly along the road, and she told her to go in and sing to them again. She was not at all unwilling, and walked along the path up to the door smiling and unfastening her loose coat as she went, so as to be ready to take it off. George Curle came to the door. She looked up at him, and indicating with a wave of her arm the direction in which Mrs Curle had gone down the hill she said, "She told me to come."

George took her into the drawing-room without letting her take off her coat. Mr Premiss was there and Olivia and Eleanor. When Mr Premiss looked up from his book and saw her coming in, he began to laugh simply from amusement at her, and he put the book down and came across the room.

"We are very, very, very glad to see you," he said. "Are you going to sign for us?"

She smiled and nodded.

Eleanor jumped up from her chair. "That's fine. We were wondering how to amuse ourselves. At least, I was. Will you come and take off your coat?"

Pauline began to push it off her shoulder, and Mr Premiss took hold of both sleeves and pulled it off. Pauline did not sit down, but stood as if waiting to begin singing at once.

"Have you brought any music?" asked Eleanor, seeing her hands empty.

"No," said Pauline smiling.

"We shall be able to find something you know," said Olivia, going to the piano.

"What songs do you know?" asked Premiss, coming into the room after hanging her coat up.

"Only what we sing in church," she said.

"Some Bach," he said to Olivia.

Pauline stood waiting while they found the book, and then Premiss came to her to find out which ones she knew.

"I know that one," she said as he turned over the pages, and she indicated with a movement of her head that he had passed the place. Her hands she kept behind her back; they were cold and a bit blue because she had worn no gloves.

He looked at her and laughed again as though he could not at all restrain his amusement. She smiled back unperturbed by it. Then he took the music to Olivia and went to sit down. It gave him immense pleasure to hear the voice of Bach's Virgin come from Pauline's lips. When she had ended he ran to the piano saying excitedly, "Play it again." Pauline looked across at Olivia, waited for the opening bars, and sang it once more.

Afterwards she sat down. Eleanor tried to talk to her, but she did not answer. She smiled her rather scornful smile, not at all embarrassed, which was her substitute for conversation in delicate situations. Olivia sat and looked out of the window at the grey sky, and George was standing in the middle of the carpet talking. After some time Olivia came up to her chair and smiling down at her said, "Will you come with me a moment?"

Pauline got up, thinking that she had to go, looking side-ways at Mr Premiss, who was, however, looking out of the window with an abstracted expression on his face and his fore-head slightly wrinkled. She followed Olivia out of the room. Olivia took her upstairs to her own room, without speaking. Here it was cold, and the grey sky outside, where it was already getting dark, seemed to have sent some of its own greyness into the room. Olivia made Pauline sit down in an armchair by the side of the little dressing-table, and she herself opened the wardrobe and began looking among her dresses. Pauline looked at the bottle of perfume on the dressing-table with the profoundest interest. She took out her handkerchief from her pocket, and said, scarcely looking at Olivia, "Can I have some of your scent on my handkerchief?"

Olivia came from the wardrobe with an orange-coloured frock on her arm. She put it down on the bed and came to the dressing-table.

"Do you like perfume?" she asked.

"Yes," said Pauline.

Olivia took up the bottle, and Pauline held out her handkerchief with both hands. Olivia shook a little of the perfume on to it and looked at her, thinking that it would be unpleasant to have so much, but Pauline was watching each precious drop so intently that she put some more until the middle of the handkerchief was quite wet. She put the light on and called Pauline to the bed. The orange-coloured dress, which had a wide frilled skirt of tulle, lay on the bed as it if were an orange cloud floating there.

"Would you like to have this dress?" said Olivia. "I don't know whether it will suit you, and it will certainly be too long; and look," she held up the skirt and showed a tear in the tulle, "do you think you can mend that?"

"It doesn't show," said Pauline.

"Would you like it?" asked Olivia. I thought you could wear it when you go to sing anywhere. It is not very old, you know, only it is a little torn there, and it is a colour that one gets tired of, though I like it very much. Will you have it?"

"I've got to sing on Boxing-night," said Pauline; "can I take it home with me now?"

"Yes, of course," said Olivia. "We will go downstairs and find some paper to pack it up in. Will you carry it?"

Pauline picked it up from the bed and began to walk out of the room. Olivia stood waiting to put out the light and looking at her. At the door she turned round and said, "Thank you, *and* for the scent."

At the bottom of the stairs she stood holding the dress, while Olivia went to find some paper to wrap it in. Mr Premiss came from the drawing-room, and seeing her standing there, turned on the light and came up to her.

"What is that?" he asked.

"A dress. She gave it to me."

"Let me see," he said, and he held it up in his hand. Olivia came out from the kitchen.

"Was this yours?" Premiss asked with interest.

"Yes," said Olivia smiling.

"And did you wear it?" he asked, looking from the dress to her to judge of the effect.

"Yes," she said. "Do you like it?"

"But what a pity you have not worn it for me to see," he said, holding out his hand for the paper, and he began very carefully packing it up on a chair.

Pauline put on her thick coat and, with the parcel under her arm, went in to say good-bye to Eleanor and George. Then she went home, and when she passed through the kitchen she had it under her coat so that her mother should not see it, and then she took it upstairs to her bedroom and hid it. Not until her mother had gone to bed would she have a chance to try it on without being caught. She had only a small mirror in her room, but she got out her best white petticoat and put on the frock. It was too long, but she found a piece of black ribbon and tied it up. Feeling the need of admiration, she went to the bed and shook Alexander, keeping one finger on her lips, because she was still a little afraid that her mother could hear. He opened his eyes in sleepy astonishment.

"Look," she said. "Mind you don't tell."

He sat up in bed and watched her walking about the room in the extraordinary bright colour. He was still too sleepy to say a word, but his wonder made his eyes wider and wider. After a bit she took it and the petticoat off. Again exhorting Alexander to secrecy, she put her dress in the large box by the window. He watched it, as it were, floating at the top of the box until the cover went down over it. Pauline arranged the old curtain which was over the box very carefully, and the turning round and seeing Alexander still blinking his eyes and looking as if he were sorry that it was no longer there to see, she evidently felt that his genuine admiration should have some reward, and taking out of her pocket the scented handkerchief, she went up to the bed and held it to his nose. He smelt it, looking up at her over it, and when she began to take it away he put his hand up to keep it there for still another moment. She opened the top drawer of the chest of drawers, and taking out all her handkerchiefs wrapped them round it one by one. Then afterwards she went to bed and they both fell asleep.

Next morning she waited until her mother was busy downstairs and then went up to Mr Nettle's bedroom where there was a large mirror. She fetched the dress from its hiding-place and carefully shut the door. She threw it on the bed while she undressed. One could imagine very well how it must have suited Olivia, because her hair was so dark. It rested on Nettle's bed like something strange and not altogether belonging to the place. Pauline found some pins in the drawer and fixed it to fit her.

Several times during the day, when it was back in the box, Alexander went upstairs to look at it and touched it reverently with his fingers and shut the box carefully, and he never said a word about it to anyone. She had not told him where she had got it from, so he thought that it came, like the chocolates, from the two gentlemen.

What is amusing is, that even on Mr Premiss, the orange-coloured frock had made an impression, because on the grey colourless day on which he had seen it, it had appeared as something quite individual in itself, quite independent of its wearers. He amused himself by picturing Olivia in it, with her round pale face and her large childlike, rather sad eyes, and he laughed to himself at the thought of Pauline with her hair of no particular colour serenely unperturbable in these incongruous feathers. But he was really quite enchanted with the little dress itself, and could have fancied himself flirting gently with it behind the backs of its two mistresses. He was sitting, thinking this, and, when Olivia happened to come into the room, he stretched his arm over the back of the chair, took her hand and, looking up at her reproachfully, said again, "Ah, you should have let me see you in that beautiful dress."

Letting her hand rest in his, she looked down and smiled very faintly. "Did you like it?" she said.

"Oh, yes," he answered smiling; "it is my ideal dress. You know that some men have their ideal woman? Well, I have my ideal dress."

He dropped her hand and put his on the back of his chair. She stopped smiling, but did not move away and stood looking down at him.

"Some day," he said, "you will see a notice in the paper – Betrothed: Mr David Premiss, the distinguished essayist, to an orange-coloured dress. The marriage is to take place quietly in a registry office. Only the relatives of the bride will attend."

"And will there be nobody inside the dress?" said Olivia, beginning to smile, but stopping rather anxiously to see if he found the remark amusing.

"I am afraid not," said Premiss, a little absent-mindedly, for he had suddenly thought how nice a girl who was half-way between Olivia and Pauline Clark, without really resembling either, would be, and he pictured her to himself, and smiled, so that Olivia could not help seeing that he was no longer attending to her; and looking at him again, she turned away and went out of the room.

Premiss would have been very pleased to spend a lot of his time walking about in the country and talking with George and his cousins, but he had come there with the serious intention of finishing a certain amount of work, so that it was often quite a matter of chance when he had a solitary conversation with any one of them. But one morning, as he was going to the post-office, he found Eleanor in the garden, and she went down with him. She had picked up a stick, and she walked near the side of the road, poking it here and there into the hedgerow. Premiss walked in the road looking at her with a smile.

"Do you know what you remind me of, Miss Eleanor?" he said.

"No," she said smiling a little suspiciously, but with curiosity.

"Of a schoolgirl dressed up as a Bacchante for the school concert."

"I assure you that they don't have Bacchantes in their concerts in girls' schools," said Eleanor; "it shows that you know nothing about it."

"It is quite true that I was never sent to a girls' school," said Premiss, laughing at this remark of his.

"And why not a real Bacchante?" asked Eleanor, half laughing.

"You haven't the right temperament," he said. "Now, I'll tell you who has the temperament of one – that girl who comes to sing."

"Pauline Clark!" said Eleanor, in surprise and disappointment. "But she is so sort of self-confident; I am sure she could never get into an ecstasy about anything."

"No; you are quite right," said Premiss, shaking his head gravely as though it were a matter of deep regret to him. "The days of Bacchantes are over and will not return. Pauline Clark won't be ecstatic, and you only get into ecstasies over ideas."

"Do I?" said Eleanor, opening her eyes wider.

He looked at her and began to laugh.

"I don't think you need always laugh at me," she said, turning away a little vexed.

"No, really, Miss Eleanor," he said, coming to her side of the road and taking her arm. "Suppose you look at that tree and try to see it, apart from any symbolical value it may have, as a material thing in all the beauty of its sheer objectivity, the lovely lines of its branches, and the hard and yet yielding solidity of its trunk, so different from a stone. You can appreciate it from that point of view, can't you?"

They stood together at the side of the road looking up at the tall tree with its naked branches stretching out far above them against the sky. Eleanor nodded her head. Premiss turned to her to see that she was attending.

"But can you get into a real ecstasy about it? No," he said emphatically.

"Perhaps, if we had drunk a lot of wine, we could," she said, looking at him seriously with her blue eyes.

"No, it doesn't have that effect at all," he said smiling, and beginning to walk on. "Do you know, Miss Eleanor, there is only one material thing about which I could really go into an ecstasy."

"What is that?" asked Eleanor, who was really very much excited by this new point of view.

"Your blue eyes," he said.

She frowned and looked down on the ground.

"Only perhaps, after all, they are really symbols, only heaven alone knows what they are symbols of. Dear me, dear me," said Premiss, walking on, and saying the last part of the remark as if he were talking to himself.

Eleanor looked at him. She was a bit annoyed. She decided not to speak to him for the rest of the walk, but as they came through the village she saw Pauline Clark walking along in front of them, and she forgot this vow, and said, "Oh, look, there is your Bacchante!"

Pauline looked round as they came up behind her. She smiled at Premiss, and let her eyes rest too on Eleanor. Premiss laughed.

"Good morning," said Eleanor. "Are you going shopping?" Pauline nodded.

Eleanor smiled at her. "We are only going to the post-office," she said.

The three of them walked on together. Pauline looked up again at Premiss and grinned. Eleanor looked from her to him to see what it was that she was laughing at. But Premiss only smiled at her and said nothing. Pauline passed the shop where she was supposed to go, and went on with them without saying anything. When they reached the post-office, Premiss went in. Pauline and Eleanor stood on the pavement outside. Eleanor looked at her with curiosity. She did not seem to her at all like a Bacchante. She could not imagine her with grapes bound round her head, and she wondered why Mr Premiss had said it.

"How old are you?" she asked Pauline.

Pauline stopped looking in through the post-office door, and said, "Seventeen last birthday."

Eleanor looked about her for something else to say. "I hope you will come to sing for us again," she said; "we all think that you have a charming voice."

Pauline smiled without embarrassment. "Is he your sister's young man?" she asked, moving her head in the direction of Premiss.

"Good heavens, no!" said Eleanor, in surprise. "He is the friend of my cousin; he is only staying with us. He is very clever," she added impressively.

Pauline made a grimace which might have been intended to show that she was indeed impressed or that cleverness seemed to her an ambiguous property.

"He is awfully nice, you know," said Eleanor, feeling that Pauline was not appreciative.

Premiss came from the post-office.

"Your friend Mr Nettle is not there," he said.

"Isn't he?" said Eleanor; "I wonder why."

"He's ill in bed," said Pauline suddenly, standing on the pavement and reluctantly watching them turning away.

"Oh, but how dreadful," said Eleanor. "Is he very ill?"

"I don't know," said Pauline.

"We must tell George to call," she said to Mr Premiss as they walked away. "I do hope it isn't serious."

Pauline watched them going down the street, and then she slowly followed them until she came to the shop where she was supposed to go.

The next morning, watching from Nettle's window, she again saw Mr Premiss walking past the house. As she put on her coat she heard her mother coming from the kitchen, and she ran quickly out of the front door to follow him. Her mother just saw her disappearing.

"Come back this minute," she shouted in extreme anger, and was answered only by the slamming of the door. She hurried outside and called after her up the street, but Pauline did not turn her head, and ran down the road on the left. The only other person to be seen was Mr Premiss, but he was already far up the road, and, since Pauline had turned in another direction, her mother did not notice him very particularly. She went into Mr Nettle's room. There was no need to lay the fire, because he was in bed and not likely to come down to-day, and Pauline had already cleared out the grate. Leaving everything in the kitchen undone, Mrs Clark sat in Nettle's room by the window and waited for her to return.

Alexander came downstairs, and after sitting on the bottom stair lacing his boots, came to the door to find her.

"Go and get your breakfast," she said to him angrily.

Alexander, withdrawing at once, went into the kitchen. He could pour his milk out himself, and he drank it and ate many spoonfuls of jam, and then sat at the table docilely and with something of the air of a martyr, waiting for some one to cut the bread.

When Mrs Clark had been sitting there for some time at the window she saw Pauline come down the road. Premiss was walking quite near her, but he was hurrying, and she lagging a little behind, so that he had half turned his head to say something to her, and she was smiling up at him. They came to the house, and he hurried on, leaving her standing on the pavement looking after him until he waved his gloved hand, and she turned reluctantly to the door and came in.

She took off her coat and was hanging it up when her

mother, coming out of the room, slapped her across the side of her head, and said, "Where've you been, you slut?"

Pauline, with her head tingling, shrugged her shoulders angrily and went in to the kitchen. Alexander, sitting patiently at the table, looked up at them with large, solemn eyes, and calculated the chances of his onslaught on the jampot not being discovered.

"Where've you been?" repeated Mrs Clark.

"For a walk," said Pauline sulkily.

"Who was that you were with?"

Pauline did not answer.

"You'd better tell me," said her mother in a quiet threatening voice.

"I only met him a minute ago," said Pauline, with sulky indignation.

"Don't you dare tell me that, you little liar. I saw you going out after him. Who is he?"

Pauline shook herself and leaned up against the wall. "It's a visitor up at the Nerans."

Mrs Clark sat down in a chair beside the fireplace. "You'll come to a bad end," she said quietly.

Pauline laughed.

"What have you been doing out all that time with him?" her mother said, looking at her with suspicious and anxious fury.

"Nothing," said Pauline, sitting down at the table and beginning to cut some bread.

"Aren't you ashamed of yourself?"

Pauline raised her eyebrows and shrugged her shoulders.

"Tell me this minute where you've been," said Mrs Clark, suddenly pushing her away from the table.

"Nowhere," shouted Pauline, losing her temper.

"You mark my words; you'll get into trouble some day," said her mother, clenching her hands so tightly that her nails dug into the palms, and looking at Pauline in desperation and despair. "You're like your father, that's what you are. No daughter of mine ought to behave like that."

"What did my father do?" asked Pauline, looking her straight in the eyes, and smiling impudently, because she knew very well.

Her mother bit her lip and got red. "Never you mind what your father did," she said; "he's dead now."

Pauline smiled her disbelief, and her mother, becoming suddenly more angry than she had been before, slapped her face with all her force. Pauline clenched her teeth and moved a step forward, but thinking better of it, she put her elbows on the table and began to cry. At first she cried quietly, wiping her tears with the bottom of her pinafore.

"Aren't you ashamed of yourself?" said her mother, looking down at her.

"What have I done?" shouted Pauline, beginning to sob.

Her mother began to cut the loaf. "Here's this poor child going without his breakfast all through you, and never saying a word."

Pauline went on crying. And by and by, as she thought of what she was getting this row for, just for going out, she began to cry loudly, with her mouth open like a child. And from sobbing with anger she began to sob from real unhappiness, and a tragic kind of feeling at the contrast between this and the early morning, when Mr Premiss had laughed and talked with her. She sat there for most of the morning, until her eyes were red, and then she went up to her room and sat on her bed and ate some of her chocolates, to make her feel happy again.

As she went downstairs Mr Nettle, hearing someone, called out from his room, but Pauline shook herself and did not answer, or go to him. He lay there, looking up at the ceiling, and listening to the clock striking off the hours.

In the afternoon George Curle called. Pauline took him into the sitting-room, and he sat down there with an expression of gravity on his face, while Pauline went upstairs to see if Mr Nettle could see him. She peeped in through the door and, since he made no sound or movement, she went downstairs again.

"I believe he's asleep," she said. "Shall I go and wake him?"

"Oh, no, not on any account," said George, getting up to go. But he sat down again and said that he would wait a few minutes, in case he woke up.

Pauline stood with her back to the sideboard and looked at him without much interest. Indeed, she began to yawn. George preserved his expression of gravity and dignity, and tapped his fingers impatiently against his knee. He took no notice of her, in fact it did not occur to him to talk to her. So they remained silent and did not have the advantage of each other's ideas. After some time he told her to go up again to see if Nettle was awake, and finding that he was she took him upstairs to see him.

The next day, as she happened to be passing, Eleanor knocked at the door and asked how Mr Nettle was. Pauline smiled at her and said "Better," because it seemed to her the best thing to say, and Eleanor smiled back at her, and did not ask anything else but walked on, and Pauline shut the door.

Nettle lay all the time in bed scarcely moving. He did not feel unhappy, although he was at first disappointed that he had not succeeded in keeping well here. All the ideas and thoughts that had worried him before seemed to have gone from his head, and if, for instance, he was thirsty and wanted a drink of water, the sensations of stretching out his hand for it and then slowly sipping it over the cold rim of the glass seemed to take up all his attention and to give him a quite distinct feeling of what one is obliged to call pleasure. If anyone came to see him he did not talk, he smiled because he felt grateful to them for coming, but he no longer felt the necessity of carrying on a conversation. Sometimes in the evenings he became very hot and tossed from side to side on his pillow and could not sleep. But in the morning he slept, and very often in the day too. Only once when his uncle had been there and told him that he would be up and about in a day or two, this affected him so much that as soon as he was alone again the tears began to roll down his cheeks at the thought of having to expend so much energy even in the future. Alexander came in to see him once, and stood looking at him, overawed by his being ill and in bed, though not shy of him himself. Nettle gave him some grapes which George had brought, and he took them and went away. So that after that Nettle lay in peace.

Olivia did not call to see him or even inquire about him, since she always heard how he was from George, and she was not like Eleanor, who believed that it was impolite even to pass the house without calling to ask at the door, or at least casting a concerned glance up at the windows. Olivia went in these days for walks by herself, thinking and even dreaming as she went along between the delicate black lacework of the leafless hedges under the soft grey sky, or she sat in the house with her hands lying idle on her lap, not reading or doing anything. Mr Premiss sometimes, looking up from his book, was a little struck with her rather subdued beauty, which seemed to him to go very well with everything around, but he did not allow these thoughts to be seen on his face, and anyone else in the room would have believed simply that he was fixing some idea more carefully in his mind when he looked up like that from his work.

There came some rather nice fine days, with a blue sky and white clouds floating across it. It was still cold, and the sun shone too faintly to light up the bare fields and the grey naked trees, but the blue sky itself seemed very beautiful. Olivia did not stay in any more. She went down between the grey hedges and under the grey bare trees through which the lovely blue sky was always visible. She felt happy. It seemed as if a new life were beginning, as though the blue sky were the beginning of spring and not only a pause in the cold greyness of the winter. She began to walk always more quickly, scarcely thinking, but hurrying on with a sensation of happiness, inexplicable and filled with that certainty of its lasting for ever, which comes just before it begins to die again.

She heard someone calling behind her and she looked round. Mr Premiss was coming along the road after her. Her heart suddenly began to beat a little quicker as she waited for him. He came up smiling.

"I have been trying to catch you up for miles," he said, "but every time I got nearer you walked more quickly than ever, and I was left behind again. If I had not been sure that you had not seen me, I should have retreated sorrowfully in another direction."

She had been looking at the ground, and she looked up at him and said, "No, it is true that I did not see you."

"No, really," he said seriously. "It was like a magic spell. I felt as though some wicked fairy was keeping the distance between us always the same. No effort of mine seemed to be any good. But then I thought of the magic word to say, and the spell was broken."

"What was it?" she asked smiling.

"What was what?" he said.

"The magic word that you said."

He reflected for a moment.

"It was 'Miss Olivia,' I believe. Wasn't that what I called?"

"I don't know; I only heard your voice, and not what you said."

"Yes, I think it was," he said gravely, and then smiled and added, "You see, your name has power against evil things."

She looked down at the ground again.

"And now," he said, "having gone through such dire and terrible adventures to reach you, may I come for a walk with you? It is really too nice a day even to work."

"Yes," she said, beginning to move on.

They did not hurry now, but walked slowly together; and when they were passing a place where, a little higher than the road, some fir trees grew, from which there was a rather beautiful view of the surrounding country, Premiss took her arm and said, "Is it too cold for us to sit there for a minute or two?"

"Not for me," she said, letting him lead her there.

He felt the ground with his fingers. "I don't think it is damp," he said, "but you had better sit on my coat," and he began to take it off.

"No, no," she said quickly. "It hasn't rained lately, and you will die of cold, and it would be my fault." She smiled.

He put on his coat again laughing, and he said, "If I suddenly died of cold here, you would have to fasten me to a stick and drag my body home along the roads and lanes down which I pursued you almost in vain. That would be a dramatic end to the fairy story." He sat down beside her and they were silent for a few moments. The branches of the fir trees rustled a little in the light wind, and the white soft clouds floated almost motionless in the sky.

On Premiss the effect of the nice weather was not to make him so especially happy. He felt a bit tired of work, and was glad to sit up there in peace for a little. Olivia sat with her hands on her lap looking down at the ground, but with her whole soul as it were stretching up like a flower to the blue sky. Premiss looked upwards, with his forehead rather wrinkled and said, "I shall be really awfully sorry if it rains again."

She looked up at him, smiling a little at his gravity.

"Will it matter to you such a lot?" she asked, "because I don't think it will always be fine like to-day; I mean, not for the rest of time."

He turned to look at her in surprise, and then seeing that she was smiling he laughed a little.

"You are a fearful person," he said, stretching out his hand and taking hers. "One never feels safe in your company."

This remark was unexpected. She looked down at her hand lying in his.

"Why?" she said softly.

"Why, because you are so critical. It is very beautiful to have a critical sense, but I am sorry when you use it on me."

She looked up at him, surprised and disappointed by the remark, because it was not in any way true, and did not in the least describe her character. She drew her hand out of his, and this made him look down at it, when he remarked with interest, "What beautiful hands you have."

She smiled at him a little faintly.

"Very beautiful hands," he repeated, looking again at the sky.

They did not speak for a few minutes, but then she said, "It is a little cold."

He got up and helped her to her feet. When they were down on the road he looked up at the place where they had sat and said, "How nice that was to sit there together and talk. We won't forget it. Every time you pass here again you try to think of me, and I will think of you every time I see a fir tree."

She did not answer.

He put his arm through hers and said, "You don't believe that I shall remember you?"

"No," she said in a much quieter voice than she had intended, raising her large dark eyes to look at him.

Instead of protesting he laughed at her, and slowly taking his arm out of hers he walked on at her side. He was smiling to himself. She felt for some reason hurt by his smile, though it may not have had anything to do with her.

The sky was becoming filled with white clouds, so that the sun no longer shone even faintly on the grey trees and the bare cold fields. Olivia looked about her with her large, rather childlike but sad eyes. Her happy mood had gone in some way; she did not feel so full of energy. There is something, too, rather unpleasant about winter; it is cold and frozen and nothing seems to move, and yet there is no sense of rest anywhere.

CHAPTER 3

Towards evening the sky became very cloudy; great white clouds covered it, and after them came thunderclouds of dark grey and purple. The rain began to beat down, and there was thunder and flashes of lightning which lit up the bare earth and the naked leafless trees.

The thunder, or the heavy warm atmosphere of a storm, always gave Olivia a headache. She lay down in her room in the dark, and, without closing her eyes, looked towards the window at the quite black night, until a flash of lightning lit up everything, and she turned away her eyes, dazzled by it. She did not stay there all the evening, but went downstairs. The thunder was less violent, but the rain did not slacken off, but beat down outside against the trees and the windows. She was still pale, and her headache was not quite gone. She picked up a book, but she scarcely read it, and often looked up from it wearily at the others – at George leaning forward eagerly to make some very urgent remark, or at Mr Premiss reading with absorption, sitting quietly on his chair. Besides her headache, she felt rather depressed now.

This feeling of depression, though it was slight, was still there the next day. The storm was over; here and there some broken branches hung down from the trees, and everything was dripping with rain, but it was not actually raining, and the sky had gone back to its usual dull grey, without movement or change.

It was already Christmas Day. It was difficult to feel festive. Mr Premiss did not judge it necessary to stop work, and Eleanor wanted to begin at once a book which one of them had given her. But George decided to go and call on Mr Nettle, and Olivia walked down to the village with him. She left him at Nettle's door, and went on by herself for a walk. The church bells were ringing, and the shops were closed, and the children were in their best clothes, as on Sundays. The bells rang because a baby had once been born who was to save the world. When she returned from her walk they were already in church; she could hear them singing. She looked at Nettle's window and wondered if George had already started for home, but instead of stopping to see, she went slowly on up the hill.

Quite late on the day after, Mr Premiss, suddenly getting tired of work, insisted on taking a walk through the village, and he made Eleanor and Olivia and George go with him. It was a cold frosty night, but the stars were out. Mr Premiss was in a very good mood; he came to Olivia's side in the dark as they went down the hill, and pushed his arm through hers, and felt with his fingers her hand inside her woollen glove.

"Oh, but they are cold," he said, looking into her eyes and smiling. "Feel how cold her hands are," he said seriously to George, and he took off his fur-lined gloves and put them on her hands over the others. She laughed as he tried to pull each finger tightly on. They were too small; but as she held out her hands for him to take them off again, he put his into his pockets and ran down the hill to Eleanor, who had walked on in front.

"But, Mr Premiss, you will be cold," Olivia called after him. "Please take them back."

"No," he shouted back, "I have a special method of keeping warm," and he put one hand into the pocket of Eleanor's coat and walked by her side.

"What are you thinking of, Miss Eleanor?"

"Nothing," said Eleanor smiling.

"Oh, come. That is not possible – to think of nothing."

"Well," she began seriously, "I was wondering if love really was so important that all the books one reads have to be about it." She looked at him with her blue eyes.

Premiss smiled, but answered seriously, "Well, love causes a lot of suffering, and when people suffer they are more interesting."

"But don't other things cause suffering too?" she said.

"Comparatively speaking, no," said Premiss, looking straight into her eyes and laughing. "No, seriously. To be loved too much, that is very unpleasant; and not to be loved enough, that is also very unpleasant. You don't love me enough."

Eleanor frowned a little, but she did not want him to stop talking about this interesting subject, so she said very gravely, "Do you think it is true that 'each man kills the thing he loves'?"

"There is something in your pocket," he said, with an air of discovery, instead of answering her question. "Oh, oh, a love-letter. Shall I read it?" and he took it out, ran on a few steps, and pretended to be trying to read the envelope by the light of the stars.

Eleanor was annoyed at being interrupted, and she felt too that he was treating her like a child, so she said in a vexed voice, "It isn't a love-letter, Mr Premiss. You can read it if you like; it is from a girl friend of mine."

Premiss looked back at her rather inattentively, waited until she came up to him, and then presenting the letter to her with a theatrical gesture of disbelief, said "I see that I shall never suffer because you love me too much," and then ran quickly before her down the hill, because he was tired for the moment of talking, and wanted to walk by himself.

He went along with his hands in the pockets of his coat, looking up at the stars in the soft dark grey sky, and he remained quite lost in his own thoughts until he came to the village, where he stood in the road before the church and waited for the others to come. From behind the church came the sound of music, and he said he wanted to see what was going on. He disappeared through the churchyard gate, and when he reappeared he was making mysterious signs, urging them to follow. They went with him round to the hall at the back.

"What is there?" whispered Eleanor.

He laughed softly. "The orange dress that your sister gave to Pauline Clark," he said. "Come and see."

He looked through the glass of the door, and then slightly opened it. He touched the arm of a boy sitting near the door and said urgently, "Please ask Pauline Clark to come here at once."

Pauline was sitting at the other end of the hall. She had fastened a black velvet ribbon round the dress, to give it a high waist, so that with all its startling colour it nevertheless had the effect of showing how young she was. When the boy gave her the message she looked suspiciously at the door, thinking that by some mischance her mother had sent for her to come home, but when she saw Premiss she smiled a little scornfully and came out to him.

"Look," he said, making her stand in front of the door for the others to see her. She stood smiling. Olivia smiled at her. The dress, although it had ceased to look as if it had ever belonged to Olivia, had not succeeded in reconciling itself with Pauline. It looked strange and as though it could never belong to her hair with its undistinctive colour. They were two interesting but incompatible personalities, the dress and Pauline, thought Premiss.

"You will catch cold," said Olivia, turning to go.

"Have you been singing?" asked Eleanor.

"Yes," said Pauline.

They turned away and Premiss pretended to follow them, but he still held Pauline's hand behind him, and when he relinquished it he turned round, and laughed down at her so that she waited there. When they got to the church he said urgently, "Just wait one moment, please," and he hurried back to the door, where he found Pauline still waiting. He made her come to the side, just out of the light, and put his arm round the waist of the frock and kissed her. He waved his hand to her as he went away, and hurried smiling to join the others, who were waiting for him at the gate. Olivia was leaning against the pillar. She looked at him a little with curiosity. He began to laugh, and putting his arm through hers, led her across the road.

"Do you think that is Mr Nettle's light?" he said, looking up at the house.

"I expect so," she said.

"Let's serenade him," said he. "I will sing a carol."

"No," said Olivia anxiously; "you know he has been ill; we should disturb him."

"Yes, really, you can't do that," said George, alarmed. "He only got up to-day for the first time."

"But then I shall certainly have to call on him to-morrow," said Premiss, with an air of slightly offended virtue, "because I haven't wished him a merry Christmas."

"It is too late for that anyhow," said Olivia.

Premiss looked regretfully at the window, but he gave up the idea and looked around to see if there was anything else he could do. His inventiveness failing him, with one hand on Olivia's arm, and slipping the other through Eleanor's, he turned and led them up the hill to the house.

And the next day, to their surprise, he did indeed insist on paying a visit to Nettle, and took Olivia and George with him. It happened, though, that they found little Alexander Clark sitting on the doorstep.

"Hullo," said Premiss.

Alexander looked up at him with large, serious eyes.

"What are you doing here?" asked Premiss.

"I live here," said Alexander.

Premiss looked round at Olivia and George in astonishment.

"Well, now, how extraordinary that is," he said in accents

of the deepest surprise. "I have passed this house dozens of times, and I always had the feeling that someone very important lived here. Wasn't that funny?"

Alexander looked at him solemnly.

"Does anyone else live here besides you?" asked Premiss.

"Yes," said Alexander.

"And if you did not allow them to, they would have to go and live somewhere else, wouldn't they?"

Alexander looked at him doubtfully, but answered "yes" again.

"Who else did you say lived here?"

"My sister and my mother and Mr Nettle."

"Is Mr Nettle in?" asked George, politely, but rather disliking to waste so much time.

Alexander nodded, but turned his attention back to Premiss immediately. George knocked at the door, and when it was opened he and Olivia went in. Premiss followed them, but carried on his conversation with the little boy until he was actually in Nettle's room.

Nettle was pleased to see them again. He smiled and shook hands awkwardly with Premiss and sat down in the chair next to Olivia. But the conversation did not go on very well, because Premiss sat on the corner of his chair, and let his attention wander to every sound that he heard in the passage; and Nettle, instead of talking to Olivia and George, looked at him in shy curiosity.

Premiss laughed as he saw the knob of the door turn round. The door did not open and the knob turned quietly back to its first position. But after a short time it turned again, and this time Alexander came half into the room.

George, who was in the middle of saying something rather important, went on speaking, but turned his eyes to the door, a little annoyed.

"Come here," said Premiss. He turned to Nettle. "Here is a young gentleman who has just informed me of the esteem and affection he has for your character. You allow him in, don't you?"

Nettle looked confused and did not answer, and his eyes met the equally surprised look of the little boy.

"Come along," said Premiss, and Alexander, still looking at Nettle, advanced into the room, until he was standing in front of Premiss's knees, and Premiss had taken his hand. Olivia looked at them.

Premiss with raised eyebrows and a very important air was saying, "Do you know who first mentioned you to me?"

Alexander, with his eyes wide open, shook his head.

"The man who lives at the South Pole. Isn't that an extraordinary coincidence?" Premiss appealed to the company generally.

Nettle, leaning back, rather white, with a tired look on his face, smiled a little, but nobody responded, not even George, who was leaning forward in his chair, with his mouth open, waiting to say something else.

"The man who lives at the South Pole only likes people like myself and you," said Premiss. "When I saw you I could see at once that you were the kind of person he likes. What do you think of that?"

Alexander, still looking at him solemnly, with an attentiveness which made his face mirror the exaggerated expressions of astonishment and mystery which he made, remained under the spell of the words long after this question, and realising only then that an answer was required of him, he allowed a dimple to appear in his cheek and he began to laugh.

"Ah, I am so fond of children," said Premiss, still holding Alexander's hand, but turning to the others. He saw that Olivia was smiling, and he looked at them all questioningly, thinking that perhaps he had said something to make them laugh.

"Don't you like children?" he asked Nettle.

"I don't think it is easy to understand them," said Nettle.

"But do you really like children *qua* children?" asked

George, excitedly, and even a little impatiently. "As individuals, yes, that I can understand, some of them are very interesting. But do you like them simply because they are young, simply for their state of potentiality quite apart from all consideration of what those potentialities are?" He waited attentively for an answer, but Premiss, beginning to laugh, became once more absorbed in Alexander. He whispered something in his ear, to which the little boy listened with profound gravity, and he continued to play with him until they said good-bye to Nettle and went away.

Alexander, when he went out to play after breakfast the next day, suddenly thought he would go up the road in case the gentleman who had talked to him yesterday should be somewhere about. He did not tell his mother where he was going, because he thought at the back of his mind that there would be some objection. He walked slowly up the hill, looking down at the ground in front of him. He had in his mind a very clear idea of Mr Premiss as he had looked when he was telling him about the man who lives at the South Pole. He was very intent on the journey, and did not even look up to see if Mr Premiss was coming, because he felt sure that Mr Premiss would know him and that he had only to go on walking steadily.

He must have walked past the house without recognising it, or perhaps he had in his mind a picture of the house with Mr Premiss in the garden, and so when he came there, this incompleteness prevented him from knowing it. For when he did not come in to dinner, and his mother sent Pauline to find him, she found him a long way past there, sitting down on the roadside, too tired to walk back and quite disillusioned. Pauline was not at all sorry to have to take a walk up in this direction, and, though she slapped him, she went on smiling to herself. But the slapping on top of the disappointment made him cry, and he had to be dragged along the road, her hand holding him by the wrist, crying and sometimes for a moment or two even screaming.

Pauline walked cheerfully along, taking no notice of him. She was wondering if Premiss would be outside the house, and she walked as slowly as possible, partly because she could not drag Alexander along any quicker and because she was in no hurry to get home. Outside the gate of the house she met Olivia. She smiled up at her. Olivia was rather surprised to be greeted at once by Alexander's screams and Pauline's serene smile.

"What is the matter with him?" she asked.

Pauline shrugged her shoulders, still smiling. "I don't know. He was running away."

"Running away!" said Olivia. "Is he your brother?"

"Yes," said Pauline.

Alexander stopped crying and looked at them both, almost stupefied by the accusation, which was so far from the truth. He felt vaguely that if the gentleman would only appear out of the house he would immediately explain the situation and straighten it out.

Olivia began to walk on, and Pauline, clutching him more firmly by the wrist, went too. Halfway down the hill he broke his long depressed silence and began to scream again, and Pauline, who was now not quite so good-tempered, gave him another slap.

If Mr Premiss had known that the little boy was outside he would have been delighted to come out to see him, but he was sitting up in his room writing, and neither saw nor heard him. He had seen Pauline walking casually along the road, and if he had not been at the moment engrossed with his own ideas he might have gone out to take a walk with her, but as it was, he smiled a little to himself since he thought he knew very well why she had come, and went on writing.

But Eleanor one day met Pauline on the hill. Pauline smiled, and Eleanor did not walk on but stopped to ask how Mr Nettle was.

"Better," said Pauline smiling. She did not take a very great interest in the invalid.

Another thing she did was to look rather ostentatiously at a silver wrist-watch on her arm, so that Eleanor noticed it and, realising after a moment that it must be new, remarked, "What a pretty watch! Was it a Christmas present?"

Pauline smiled. "Yes," she said, examining it again herself.

It may be remarked that before Pauline got home she carefully took the watch off and hid it in her pocket, because it was her mother who had given it to her and she only allowed her to wear it on Sundays, whereas Pauline wanted to make sure that if she happened to meet Mr Premiss there would be a chance of his seeing it.

Eleanor reflected all the way home on Pauline's obvious pride in the watch, which was not a very expensive one and not very nice, and she went and looked in her room until she found some green beads which she felt she could give away. And she wore them after that whenever there was a possibility of her meeting Pauline. One day in the village she saw her and, first of all opening her coat so as to have the beads well in sight, she hurried towards her.

"How is Mr Nettle to-day?" she asked.

"Better," said Pauline smiling.

Eleanor looked carefully to see if she had the wrist-watch on, but she could not see it, so instead of mentioning the subject, she began to play with her beads. Pauline looked at them appraisingly but did not say anything.

"Do you like these beads?" asked Eleanor.

Pauline nodded.

"If you would like to have them," Eleanor said, leaning forward to speak more quietly and with great seriousness, "I will give them to you with pleasure, because I really haven't any dress that they go with at the moment. Would you like them?"

"Yes," said Pauline, holding out her hand.

Eleanor was a little embarrassed. "I can't give them to you here," she said; "I thought you could come up to fetch them, or I could bring them to your house."

Pauline did not say anything but she looked disappointed.

"Oh," said Eleanor apologetically, "I only meant that perhaps you would not like me to give them to you here, where people can see."

She began to pull them over her hat, and then, holding them tightly hidden in her hand and looking round her to see that no one was looking, she gave them to Pauline. Pauline took them, smiled, and began to move away. Eleanor watched her go, feeling rather disappointed that she had not thanked her. She tried to point out to herself that, after all, one needed no assurance of the pleasure that Pauline would get from them, and they were really quite beautiful, a very charming shade of green, and they made a long string.

When Pauline got home she made sure that Mr Nettle was downstairs, and went into his bedroom to get the full effect of them in the big mirror. Then she put them away with her handkerchiefs and her watch in the empty chocolate box. She never happened to show them to Alexander. She wore them when she was out in the evening, but she could easily wrap them in her handkerchief, and put them away without anyone knowing, and he did not see them, which was rather a pity, because he would certainly have admired them, and they would have had an added interest because he imagined that everything that Pauline got came from Mr Premiss.

Olivia, during these few days after Christmas, found herself plunged in a depression which she could not throw off. It may have been due partly to the rather heavy atmosphere which, even when the thunderclouds had disappeared from the sky, told that they were not far away. And often she stood in her room at the window looking at their deep purples and greys hanging threateningly above the numbed, helpless trees and the hard, frozen soil. There was a sense of expectation in the air, but an expectation that did not express hope or fear or anything particular. The grey, distorted branches of the bare trees took on, somehow, beneath this sky, an air of tragedy and a kind of endless suffering. When the storm came the rain seemed to beat down on them cruelly.

Even if it did not make so distinct an impression on everyone, there was no avoiding the depressing effect of the weather. Arnold Nettle, who was now a little better and might have gone out if the sun had shone, stayed always in the house, and felt no desire to move away, although he was conscientious, and did not like to be so long from his work.

Purple-black clouds hung over the leafless trees and the air was intolerably heavy. It looked as though another thunderstorm must come at once, but it did not, and next morning the sky was full of white-grey clouds.

George Curle walked along the road reflecting very deeply, and even with a slight frown on his face. He knocked a stone in front of him with his stick, and looked so intently on the ground that he passed Pauline Clark without seeing her at all. She turned to look after him with a half-contemptuous grimace. When he got into the house again he felt a bit vexed and, in a way, rather anxious to quarrel with someone, and since he found no one about except Premiss, whom he did not really like to disturb, he went upstairs and knocked at the door of his mother's room. She was rearranging the things in some drawers, and the room was untidy with many things lying about.

"What is it?" she said, pretending an interest which was really taken up by calculations about the arrangement of the drawers.

George looked for a chair to sit on, and moved some things carefully but a little irritably from it on to the bed. He sat down.

Mrs Curle went on tidying the drawer, and looking out of

the window as she walked back and fore, she began to hum in a very tuneless manner. George made a gesture of impatience. "Oh, don't mother," he said.

"Don't what?" she asked, surprised.

"Don't hum like that."

"Your father used to like me to sing," she said complainingly, carrying some things from a table to the drawer and taking them absent-mindedly back again.

"But it was out of tune," said George irritably.

"Your father –" began Mrs Curle, but stopped and contemplated with anxiety a pile of things that should have gone in first.

"You are nothing like your father," she said again, after a pause. "Your father had no patience. That was his fault. He used to come into the house sometimes and say 'Maria, I can't stand this life any longer.' What life he could not stand I never could find out. We were never poor. I was very pretty when I was younger. We had a very bad cook for years that we couldn't get rid of, but your father was not very fond of food. The only thing is that he was very ambitious, and that never made him do anything out of the ordinary; it simply made him impatient."

"But I must have something of him in me," said George.

Mrs Curle contemplated him in the mirror. "Yes; you've got his forehead and his nose, but otherwise you are like me. When your Aunt Martha first saw you when you were a baby she said, 'Maria, as long as that child lives you will never die.' She didn't like your father. She always said that he used to laugh at her. He laughed at all my family."

"It's a curious thing," said George beginning to feel a bit depressed but somewhat losing his bad temper, "to feel oneself as it were on the background of two distinct families. I wish I had known some of my father's people, too."

"Your father hadn't any people," said she. "Your Aunt Martha always used to say 'Beware of a man, Maria, who comes to you like a bolt from the blue, without any connections. He may have a wife somewhere else! But as a matter of fact, your father never proposed to me. He carried me by storm."

George smiled.

She looked at him reprovingly. "But that isn't the right way. I think there ought to be an engagement, not too long, but just a nice time for them to get to know each other better. And it is much nicer for the girl to have time to get her things together. I know how I spent the first months of my married life sewing."

George suddenly sighed deeply.

"You are just the sort of man who ought to be careful," said his mother. "You ought never to marry without letting me see her first, because you are no judge of character. You take a fancy to people and then you get sick of them."

"Nonsense," said George irritably, and feeling at once very angry again. "You think I have taken a fancy to people when I am merely interested in them for their conversation. A wife," he began to stammer a little, "is something quite different."

"It's always the same," she said, without being astonished at his indignation. "Young people never take advice. I would never listen to your Aunt Martha, although she was much older in her ways and more staid than I."

"But I tell you that what you say is not true," said George, really quite furious, thumping his knee with his fist.

Mrs Curle looked round in surprise. "What is not true?"

"That I am no judge of character."

"But, George, look at the mistakes you have made."

"I have never made any mistakes," said George emphatically.

"You surely don't mean to say that that foolish man you met in the train and invited for the week-end wasn't a mistake, and the girl with the blue ostrich feather in her hat who came to tea."

"No," said George, almost beginning shout. "They were not mistakes. I invited them for their conversation. I got a great deal of amusement and information from both. There was no question of my wanting to marry the girl."

Mrs Curle was shocked and she said, "I should hope such a thing never entered your head."

"I am just telling you that it didn't," he said, getting up from his chair as if he were preparing to walk out of the room.

"All I am saying," said his mother in an injured tone, "is that if you have no judgement about choosing your friends, what is going to help you to choose a wife?"

"Love," said George, going out of the room and slamming the door.

She looked after him in astonishment, and then went on tidying the drawers with an expression of complaining resignation on her face. But when George turned up at dinner smiling and in the best possible spirits, either she did not remember that they had quarrelled or she did not think it worth referring to.

That evening George went out for a walk by himself in the moonlight. It was not a very beautiful romantic moonlit night because the sky was cloudy and the moon shone out of the soft clouds and had a yellow ring around it. George had, it is true, regained his good temper, but he began to think about his father, and his together with the moonlight began to have the effect of making him feel romantic. The moon shone down through the bare black branches of the trees on to the road. George went along slowly with his hands in the pockets of his coat. He was thinking that though he had many good friends, and the companionship and affection of Olivia and Eleanor, which not every man was lucky enough to enjoy, yet there comes a time when a man feels the need of feminine sympathy, something, that is to say, given to himself alone, and not shared with other people. At this moment the girl with the blue ostrich feather came into his mind and rather annoyed him, though it was a matter of no importance, and her conversation really had been interesting, or at least something quite different from what he was used to. If it had been summer he would have sat down at the roadside and looked up at the sky and followed out these reflections to their conclusion, but it was too cold even to walk, except if one hurried, so he turned and went back.

When he got to the house his mother and Mr Premiss and Eleanor were there, and he stood and listened to them before sitting down. Mr Premiss was saying, "I suffer a lot from sleeplessness, or at least I do not suffer, but I cannot sleep."

"You ought to take a glass of hot milk before you go to bed," said Mrs Curle.

"Oh, Auntie," said Eleanor deprecatingly.

Mr Premiss looked round at her in surprise. "Why, Miss Eleanor?"

"Well, drinking hot milk before you go to bed is so childish, and you are grown up."

"Yes, but Miss Eleanor," he said, smiling at her, "you don't understand. That is what I need, something that will make me like a little child, and then I shall sleep the minute I put my head on the pillow, as you do."

Mrs Curle looked at Eleanor without taking any notice of the interruption and said "But be sure you take it hot. Cold milk will keep you awake."

"Yes," said Premiss, giving her his whole attention.

Eleanor smiled ruefully and said, "Well, anyhow, I don't think it is a very romantic remedy."

Mr Premiss half-smiled and took her hand to keep her quiet while he went on talking to Mrs Curle.

George looking at them and at his mother felt a sudden wave of loyalty and affection, and he even felt a little guilty that he had been thinking so much about other women all day. He turned on his heel, took his hands out of the pockets of his coat, and, with an affectionate but dignified expression on his face, went to lean on the back of his mother's chair.

One day he met Olivia coming along the road, and he turned back to walk a little way with her. She stopped at a gate and stood there, looking across the fields, and pulling with her fingers at the dark, rather damp branches of a little tree at the side. George would have leaned on the gate but the wood was damp and he stood a few inches from it and took out his clean handkerchief and carefully rubbed his coat where it had brushed against it. He looked up again. Olivia was standing there, with her hand resting on the bare tree, quite motionless, her large dark eyes contemplating the fields in front of them quietly and sadly. Her sadness, which could not really have any cause, rather struck George at that moment. He put his hands in his pockets and, looking in front of him musingly, he said, "I suppose it is really true that women have a unique capacity for never losing sight of the element of tragedy that there is in all life."

This seemed to him to have been put nicely, so he turned to judge of its effect on her. She had turned her head and was looking at him seriously, and he saw for the first time what Mr Premiss meant when he spoke of her innocent and child-like expression, which was given her by the way her eyelashes curved upwards. He smiled at her affectionately, and she, instead of answering, smiled at him a little, and went on contemplating the fields.

"There is nothing the matter, is there?" said George anxiously, but still rather pleased at his idea about women and tragedy.

"No," said Olivia, "not particularly. I feel a little depressed, but there is no reason for it."

"I know the sort of thing you mean," said George sympathetically. "I think on the whole, you know, that depression is simply tiredness, mental or physical, or one might almost say emotional. Don't you agree?"

"I don't know," she said, sighing a little. "I think perhaps if one could learn to be absolutely receptive of every sensation and every impression as it comes, without any reference to what one expects, or to what one wants, one would be perfectly happy." She smiled a little.

George held his head a bit on one side and looked down at the bars of the gate.

"You know, that is very feminine, too," he said rather thrilled.

She smiled and took her hand from the tree. There was a brownish-green mark across it from the wet branch.

"Oh, look!" she said.

George took her handkerchief and wiped her hand.

"It is quite true that they are pretty hands," he said.

"Why do you say that it is quite true?"

"Because Premiss says that they are pretty."

She did not answer.

About this time, too, George had a conversation with Eleanor which made him feel that he was getting an insight into the workings of the feminine mind, because one of the really nice things about him was that it never occurred to him that Eleanor was perhaps too young to demonstrate this. She was reading, and he came into the room to look for something. He walked about looking for it, but she was so much absorbed in the book that she took no notice of him at all. This, of course, rather made him want to see what she was reading, and when he passed the chair he looked down over her shoulder and read:

As two whose love, first foolish, widening scope,
Knows suddenly, with music high and soft,
The Holy of Holies; who because they scoffed
Are now amazed with shame, nor dare to cope
With the whole truth aloud, lest heaven should ope,
Yet, at their meetings, laugh not as they laughed

In speech, nor speak at length; but sitting oft
Together, within hopeless sight of hope
For hours are silent: ...

"Good heavens!" said George, "what are you reading?"

"Do be quiet," said Eleanor. "Rossetti."

George did not go away, but sat down and looked at the carpet, still really quite astonished.

"Well, I have no prejudice against Rossetti," he said at length, "but that does seem to me nonsense."

"Oh, George," said Eleanor, looking up at him with serious blue eyes, "but it is really poetry. Listen." She took up the book and read aloud, –

"'but sitting oft
Together within hopeless sight of hope
For hours are silent.'

You can't say that isn't beautiful."

"But," said George laughing, "it doesn't mean anything."

"I shan't speak to you if you laugh," she said, burying her head in the book once more. "I can't quite explain in so many words what it means, but you oughtn't to be insensible to beauty."

George sat and looked at her with a broad smile on his face.

In a moment she looked up again and said, "It is called 'Known in Vain.'"

George could not contain himself any longer, but laughed very much.

"You are a beast, George," she said, turning round in her chair so as to have her back towards him, and then suddenly she put her head down on the arm of the chair and began to cry.

George got up and stood in front of her in astonishment and horror.

"Eleanor, darling. What is the matter?" he asked.

"Nothing," she sobbed.

"Have I hurt you?" he said with anxiety.

"No," she said.

"Then what is wrong?"

"Nothing," she repeated.

"But, my dear girl, there must be something the matter or you wouldn't cry like this for nothing."

She lifted her head up with tears running down her cheeks and said, "It isn't for nothing. Mr Premiss says that I am a child, and that I am incapable of love."

George was very much surprised, and rather puzzled as to what to say.

"Perhaps he was teasing you?" he said hopefully.

"No, he wasn't," said Eleanor, beginning to weep afresh.

"Well, I shouldn't mind what he said, if I were you," said George soothingly, stroking her hair with his hand.

"I don't," she said indignantly.

"Oh," said George, not altogether convinced.

Since she went on crying softly, taking no notice of him, and he did not know what to say, he went quietly out of the room. In the other room Premiss was working at the table by the window. He looked up as George came in and smiled. George looked down at him doubtfully, and then said in a reproachful voice, "Eleanor is crying."

"Why?" asked Mr Premiss in surprise.

"Well" – George for some reason felt very awkward about this – "she says that you say she is incapable of love."

"Oh, did I?" said Premiss with interest.

"But –" began George.

"It is perfectly true about all young people," said Premiss. "The whole universe is bounded for them by their own personality. They can't get outside themselves. They are as incapable of loving another person as you are incapable of loving an inhabitant of Mars. It is a very interesting and even a very beautiful phase of adolescence."

"Yes, but," said George, waving a vigorous and agitated finger in her direction, "Eleanor is crying in there now."

Premiss began to laugh, but he got up and hurried out of the room. George followed him, and found him talking to Eleanor earnestly. He was bending down to her and holding her hand in his and saying, "But you *are* a child, you see, or you wouldn't cry when I tell you what is the truth."

Eleanor did not answer, but pressed her forehead against the chair.

"Miss Eleanor," said Mr Premiss, you know you are my own darling child, of whom I am so very fond. Look up at me, and tell me that is true."

Eleanor raised her head and looked up at him. She was laughing now, though there were some tears on her cheek.

"I'm sorry," she said. "I *am* a baby."

"No," said Mr Premiss, "you are my little darling. Aren't you?"

"Yes," she said, beginning to blush a little, but smiling at him with her blue eyes. He pressed her hand gently, and turned to George, very well satisfied with himself. "You see. She has forgiven me," he said, and he hurried back to work.

But when he and George got back to his room they found that a number of papers had been blown on to the floor, and some more were following them, and this sent Mr Premiss into such a paroxysm of nerves, because he was accustomed to write on loose sheets of paper, and it was a great trouble to put them all in the right order again, that George did not dare to discuss Eleanor's state of mind with him, but hurriedly went down on his hands and knees and helped to pick up the leaves. And it was indeed only when he was picking up the last one from under the sofa, and Premiss was sorting them out, with an irritated and preoccupied expression on his pale face, that he had time to think how really extraordinary it was that Eleanor should be reading Rossetti, and that she should cry because someone had told her that she was incapable of love.

That every evening the same sort of thing happened. When it was nearly bedtime, and Eleanor stood up with her book in her hand ready to go upstairs, Mrs Curle suddenly said, quite crossly, "Please not to take that book upstairs."

Eleanor swung round. "But, Auntie, why not?" she said.

"You mustn't read in bed."

"Oh, Auntie, I'm seventeen; surely I can do as I like."

Mrs Curle did not answer.

Premiss looked up from his book and smiled. "You will spoil your beautiful eyes," he said.

Eleanor, encountering his laugh and Mrs Curle's look of obstinate decision, suddenly flung the book on the floor, and stamped her foot angrily. "I can do exactly as I like," she said.

"Eleanor, don't be stupid," said Olivia; and George looked from her to his mother rather in embarrassment.

"She is a naughty girl," said Mrs Curle, more or less to herself.

This, for some reason, made Premiss laugh, which so infuriated Eleanor that she went out and slammed the door.

Olivia frowned, and George picked up the book, but Mrs Curle did not say anything. Mr Premiss read for a few moments, and then he put down his book and went out of the room.

He looked up the stairs, but before going up he looked into the other rooms downstairs, and found Eleanor in the kitchen. There was no one there, and she was standing before the fire.

"Hullo, Miss Eleanor," he said, going up to her.

It appeared that she was really in a very bad temper; she had been clenching her hands tightly together.

"I hate her," she said.

He began to laugh.

"There is no need to laugh at me," she said; "she is very difficult to live with."

"My dear Miss Eleanor," he said smiling at her, "that is always a difficulty. The old want the young to avoid their mistakes, and the young want to make the mistakes all on their own account."

"Of course, you can only see her point of view," said Eleanor, shrugging her shoulders.

"No, I see yours very well," he said seriously. "A mistake made twenty years ago cannot be repeated. There is something new and individual in the experience, even if it means ruining those beautiful eyes."

Eleanor looked up at him with innocent attention, because this theory seemed to put her more in the right than she had really felt. Premiss began to warm his hands at the fire.

"When you come to stay in my house," he said, "you will have to go to bed at seven o'clock every night."

"Why?" she asked in surprise.

"Because eyes like yours are too dangerous to be kept open too long."

The door of the drawing-room opened and the voices of the others could be heard. Eleanor was going to say something to him again, but he shook his head mysteriously, and without saying anything more hurried her out into the hall.

He went up to his room, drank his hot milk, and began consulting his engagement book to see when it would be most convenient for him to go away, because he was already getting a little tired of staying there. He studied it for a long time without actually fixing a date, and then went to bed, and lay for hours awake in the dark.

Pauline Clark did not see him very often now, partly because her mother kept a watch on her in the mornings, but partly too because he himself did not go out so often for walks. If he got up early he began work even before breakfast. If he went down to the village she generally saw him, and if she could, she went out so that he met her and said something to her before hurrying on; but once, when she had not seen him for some days, she was not even sure that he had not gone away.

She went into Mr Nettle's room to clear the table and she said, "Is that visitor up at the Neran's gone away?"

"I don't know," said Nettle, "No, I don't think so."

She made a grimace and, not thinking it worth while to ask anything more, went out of the room.

Nettle sat looking at the fire. He thought her curiosity about Mr Premiss was rather strange. But the next time George Curle called on him he actually asked him if Premiss was still there, and afterwards, when he happened to see Pauline, he told her that he was. Pauline smiled up at him in her rather insolent way. It may have been from gratitude.

One day when Mrs Curle was passing his house she saw him in the window. He was standing there looking out. She went up and spoke to him, but since the window was closed he could not hear what she was saying and looked rather alarmed and worried, and since it did not at first occur to him to go and open the door, they stood there, rather stupidly, without being able to communicate. When at last he came to the door, she at once went in with him, because he must not stand there in the draught. He made her sit down, and since he could not offer her a cigarette he was a little embarrassed as to what he ought to do with her. She sat down heavily in his armchair and said, "I asked if you were better, but you couldn't hear me."

Nettle felt confused that he had not asked her at once what she had tried to say, as if he had no desire to hear it.

"Yes," he said. "Only not quite well enough to go back to work yet. I feel very tired."

"Don't go back until you are quite well," she said. "My husband never took any interest in his work except when he got ill, and then he suddenly insisted on going back to it before he was better, and that killed him."

"Oh," said Nettle, not knowing quite what to say. "Was he Mr Curle's father?"

"Yes," she said. "I have only had one husband. I have twice sent down something for you to eat," she added, looking round the room as if for signs of her gifts. "I hope you got them".

"Oh yes," said Nettle, embarrassed. "Mr Curle bought them, and I thought they were from him. I didn't know they were from you. Thank you."

Mrs Curle took no notice of what he was saying but looked around her. "Why don't you live with your uncle?" she asked abruptly.

"There isn't any room," said Nettle. "They live above the post-office, and the house is not very big. I prefer to be here, too," he added, looking thoughtfully at the fire. "If I want to practise I am not disturbing anybody."

"But there is somebody in the house, isn't there?" she interrupted him.

Nettle looked round him in alarm.

"Haven't you a landlady, and that insolent girl?"

"Yes," he said.

"Did they look after you when you were ill?"

"Yes," he repeated.

Mrs Clark knocked at the door, and asked if she could bring them some tea. Nettle looked up gratefully, relieved that she had thought of this.

Mrs Curle did not enter into conversation with Mrs Clark, but she stayed and had tea, and made a few remarks to Nettle which were not in themselves of importance, but which seemed to admit him to some degree of intimacy, and he, for his part, was very careful to answer all her questions and not to say anything which might offend her in any way.

When she reached home she did not take any more tea, but said she had had it with Mr Nettle, so that everyone was rather surprised, though they did not say anything beyond asking if he was better.

The next day she sent Olivia down there with something

for him. But it was fairly early in the morning and he was not yet up. Pauline went to the door. Olivia would not go in. Pauline examined the parcel carefully. She had had a vague hope that it might be something for her. But then she took it up to Mr Nettle's room.

"Miss Neran bought you this," she said.

"Is she downstairs?" he asked, looking up from the pillow.

"No, she's gone," said Pauline.

He smiled up at her without moving his head, and she put the parcel down and went out. He felt very tired, almost more than he had been since he was first ill. He thought that he must remember to thank Mrs Curle, because it must be from her, like the things that George Curle had brought, and he was rather ashamed that he had not thanked her for them.

Olivia would have called to see him if she had thought that it would give him any pleasure, but though it was a comparatively short time since he had been ill, for her lately the days seemed to have stretched themselves out endlessly, and the time seemed to move for her so slowly, like a long *adagio*, that Nettle had the place in her mind almost of someone whom she had met a few times many years before. She felt at this time a certain lassitude of mind which made her scarcely desire to talk to anyone or even to read, and she sat most of the day without moving, her hands lying idle in her lap. Or sometimes she sat sewing with Mrs Curle, and listening in an absent way to her few remarks, and doing little more than smiling in answer, or appearing to reflect upon them, by letting her work drop on her lap, and looking up at the grey sky.

Eleanor came into the room and stood at the door smiling at them. "I am going for a walk," she said; "will anyone come?"

There was no answer.

"Do come, Olivia," she said.

"No, I'm too tired," said Olivia smiling.

"Oh dear. I shall have to go by myself. Everyone else is busy, and you are too lazy." She went out again.

Mrs Curle sighed. "I remember when I was her age," she began, but instead of continuing the remark, she went on with her work. And only after a few minutes she said, "Eleanor is getting silly ideas into her head."

Olivia smiled.

"Why, Auntie, what has she done?"

"Nothing," said Mrs Curle. "She reads poetry all day."

"But I expect she likes it."

"Nonsense," said Mrs Curle; "it's silly ideas."

"She is young," said Olivia; everyone reads poetry at that age. I did. Besides, I read it now too."

Mrs Curle put on a complaining expression but did not answer.

Olivia looked through the window up at the grey sky. Some whitish-grey clouds floated across it so slowly, as to seem to hang almost motionless.

"I never liked poetry," said Mrs Curle, a long time afterwards. "Your uncle used to read it to me, when we were first married. But I never really understood what he was reading – he had a rather sing-song voice, and he gave it up after a time."

"I am sorry I never knew him," said Olivia. "He must have been entertaining."

"Yes, he was entertaining," said Mrs Curle. "Your Aunt Martha couldn't tolerate him, and he used to call your father conventional."

"I suppose he was in a way," said Olivia, and was silent again.

When George and Mr Premiss came in to drink tea George said suddenly, "It's New Year's Eve."

"When I was a girl I used to make New Year resolutions," said Mrs Curle.

"People still do it," said George, beaming on her. "I must

try and think of one to make. And where is Eleanor? She can make one not to take the bookmarks out of my books and use them for her own."

"She is out for a walk," said Olivia. "Shall you make one, Mr Premiss?"

"Make what?" he asked, because he had not been listening to what George had said.

"A New Year resolution," said George, smiling benevolently.

Mr Premiss smiled, as though the question were not worth answering, and began to help himself to more lumps of sugar in his tea.

Eleanor came in with red cheeks and her hair rather blown about.

"Can I have tea like this without doing my hair?" she asked. "I've been for a glorious walk."

She sat down and began to eat a cake, while George poured out tea for her.

"Do you know whom I met?" she said, after a minute, to Mr Premiss. "Pauline Clark!"

"Oh, did you?" said Premiss, for a moment rather embarrassed at having this information addressed only to him, and looking remarkably non-committal.

"Do you know what she said?" said Eleanor.

"No," said Premiss, beginning to smile.

"She said that her little brother stole a penny from his money-box, and when he was smacked he cried, and said that you had told him to."

"I!" said Premiss in astonishment.

"Yes. Did you?" asked Eleanor with curiosity.

"No, surely I didn't," said Premiss, beginning to laugh. "I only saw him when we called on George's friend. You were all there. I didn't say anything that could be so misinterpreted?" He looked at Olivia. "Did I?"

She turned her serious eyes on him and said, "No, I don't think so."

"The very sight of you seems to corrupt the young," said George amiably, getting up to pour out some more tea, and putting his hand affectionately on his shoulder as he passed. "I shouldn't think even Socrates had this effect on the babies in their cradles."

This observation seemed for some reason to please Mr Premiss inordinately.

"If you are taking all the credit for the corruption," said Eleanor wickedly, "it seems a pity that it was Pauline Clark's little brother who got smacked."

"Eleanor!" said George, rather horrified.

Mr Premiss laughed very much.

"That is very good. That is really very good."

"It is New Year's Eve," said Mrs Curle abruptly, looking reprovingly at Eleanor.

"Yes, I know," she said; "we have to stay up to see the New Year come in."

"You will be asleep long before," said Premiss, putting his cup down and sitting on the edge of his chair, because he wanted to go back to work.

"Do you want to stay up?" said George to Olivia.

"No," she said. "I shall go to bed in any case. I feel really extraordinarily tired. I can hear the bells from there."

Mr Premiss always found it very difficult to conceal his impatience. The minute he saw Mrs Curle looking at him, he sprang up, excused himself very politely, and ran off to his work.

When Olivia got up to go out of the room Eleanor put her arm through hers and said as they walked out, "Why won't you stay up, Olivia darling? You are mean."

"I am tired," said Olivia. "I don't know why, but I feel extraordinarily tired these days."

"You haven't a headache?"

"No."

"Are you depressed then?" said Eleanor anxiously. "Don't be depressed. I am in an awfully good mood."

"One can see that," said Olivia smiling. "No, it isn't depression at all. I am sure that if I stayed up I should simply fall asleep in the chair."

"You are not going to get ill or something, are you?"

"No."

"I do hope Mr Premiss will stop work and be amusing to-night. Do you think he will?"

"If he wants to, he will."

Eleanor took her arm away and walked off, reflecting deeply about the matter.

She watched Premiss carefully and anxiously all the evening. She did not dare to mention the subject again. But he went on working. When Olivia was already preparing to go upstairs and Eleanor had all but lost hope, he came in and said, "We must celebrate the New Year."

Eleanor's face wreathed itself in smiles. He turned to Olivia.

"You are not going to bed already?"

"Yes," said Olivia. "You must forgive me."

"Oh, Miss Olivia, you can't go," he said, taking hold of her hands. "No, really, don't go."

Olivia looked down and shook her head.

"She won't, really," said Eleanor. "I asked her before."

Mr Premiss straightened up, let go of Olivia's hands, and said good-night politely. As Olivia went out he had turned to Eleanor, and stood listening to her while she excitedly made plans.

Olivia went up to her room. She looked at herself in the mirror as she slowly took down her hair. As she was undressing she caught her hand in the little string of pearls round her neck, and it broke and they were scattered about the floor. She felt too tired to look for them, and left them to be picked up in the morning. Then she lay in the dark on her bed, looking up at the starless sky. After a time she heard Mrs Curle's heavy step on the stair. Eleanor and Mr Premiss and George were left to themselves.

She could not go to sleep, because she could not prevent herself from waiting for the bells to ring, though it was not yet time. Not long before midnight she heard the front door open and their voices in the garden. After a time only George and Mr Premiss spoke together. Eleanor must have gone away from them. Once Mr Premiss called her, but she did not answer, and they went on talking. Suddenly the bells began to ring, one after the other. She moved her head on the pillow and listened to them.

Mr Premiss began to call, "Miss Eleanor, Miss Eleanor." He became more urgent, and his voice sounded further away. Then he was silent. But a short time afterwards she heard the three voices again and they went into the house.

She closed her eyes and lay still, almost sleeping. There was nothing to keep her awake any longer. But a light knock came at her door and Eleanor came in.

"Are you awake?" she whispered.

"Yes," said Olivia, opening her eyes.

Eleanor came to her bed.

"A happy New Year," she said, kissing her. "Did you hear the bells?"

"Yes," said Olivia, not moving, but taking her hand.

Eleanor sat down on the bed without speaking.

"Did you enjoy it?" asked Olivia.

"Yes. I don't know," said Eleanor, and suddenly began to cry.

"Eleanor. What *is* the matter?" said Olivia.

"He kissed me," Eleanor sobbed.

"Who kissed you?" asked Olivia smiling.

"Mr Premiss," she said, taking her hand away, and pulling out her handkerchief.

"You are stupid, Eleanor. Of course. People always kiss after the New Year. Didn't George kiss you?"

"Yes," said Eleanor, beginning to dry her tears.

"You are getting quite hysterical," said Olivia. "You

mustn't be such a little goose. Have you been drinking wine?"

"Yes, only for healths." Eleanor blew her nose and put her handkerchief back in her pocket. She smiled at Olivia, and suddenly bent down and hugged her.

"Good-night, you darling," she said, beginning to go out.

"Don't step on my pearls," said Olivia, turning her head on the pillow. "I broke the string and I was too lazy to look for them."

"Shall I pick them up?"

"No thank you. To-morrow will do. Good-night."

"Good-night."

The door closed and Olivia lay again in the dark looking through the window at the starless heavens.

CHAPTER 4

A day or so after the New Year Mr Premiss packed up and went away in the afternoon, but that morning he took an early walk, really wishing to take leave of the countryside, and since he did not particularly want to meet Pauline Clark, he did not go the usual walk, but instead, up the hill on the other side of the village. But Pauline saw him passing from Mr Nettle's window, and she ran like a little cat so as to come out in front of him at the turning further along the road.

He smiled at her amiably when he saw her, but he walked on so quickly that she could not easily keep up with him, and lagged just a little behind. But as he reached the top of the hill and the road became level, he slackened his pace, and, suddenly arrested by the appearance of a tiny copse in the hollow at the side of the road, he stopped altogether. He stood looking at the trees, with Pauline standing beside him, wondering what could be taking his attention so completely.

But the leafless trees were indeed extraordinarily beautiful just here in all their misty colours of black, grey, brown, and sometimes a curious red. Here and there among them was the dark, deep green of fir trees which seemed to stand down there among the shades like heroes who alone can descend living into Hades. Somewhere in their midst, half concealed by their bare lifeless branches, was the wonderfully delicate green of a young fir, like a strange little maiden who had wandered by some mischance into that baneful place, like poor Persephone herself, with her beauty obscured and veiled by joyless shadows.

Mr Premiss looked at it for a long time, then he turned to Pauline. "I'm going home to-day," he said.

"Where to?" she asked.

"Oh, far away. Hundreds of miles," he answered.

She smiled a little scornfully. She did not say anything. It seemed suddenly to occur to them both that, if that were so, he would want to kiss her good-bye. He put his arm round her, round the loose thick coat, but thinking better of that, he opened her coat and slipped his arm under it round her waist and kissed her a few times. Afterwards he looked down at her, smiling, and she smiled at him. Then taking her hand and putting it with his own into the pocket of his coat to keep warm, he began to walk back with her.

When they reached the place where he had met her, she said good-bye, but she stood looking after him as he hurried away. He turned again and shouted good-bye and then she went slowly down the road. She would get a row from her mother when she got in.

During the morning Premiss had to go to the post-office. Eleanor, from her bedroom window, watched him go out of the gate and hurry down the hill. It was too late to run down and go with him. She wanted to talk to him before he went, and she was staying upstairs in her bedroom, waiting to hear the door of his room, because she thought that he was in there packing. He must have gone down very quietly, or a long time before. It was cold, but she decided to stay up there and watch for him. As soon as he came into sight on the hill she intended to go down and out of the gate as though she were going for a walk, and then, she hoped, he would perhaps go with her a little way.

He was not long. He came hurrying up the hill. She went down and got to the gate in time to meet him. She looked up at him and smiled with her blue eyes. She was unconsciously barring his way because she expected him to speak, whereas he evidently intended only to smile and hurry into the house. When she realised this, she was embarrassed, but she sud-denly thought how necessary it was that she should have a last conversation with him and she said, "I am going for a short walk. Would you like to come?"

She could not help letting an anxious and even a pleading note come into her voice. She was rather ashamed when she thought of it afterwards. He looked in uncertainty at the house and laughed doubtfully. But then he turned and went with her.

"You see, Miss Eleanor," he said in explanation, "I am a very disorderly man. I have left something in every corner of the house and it takes me a terrible time to pack. It is because I am a bachelor, you know. If I had a wife it would be all right."

"But you wouldn't let your wife do your packing for you?" said Eleanor, a little shocked by this.

"Yes, I would," he said, looking at her solemnly.

"But you couldn't let your wife be a slave to you, Mr Premiss!"

"Yes, I could," he said, highly amused.

She walked on in silence.

"Why, Miss Eleanor," he said, "you are cross with me?"

"Well, she said, gravely raising her eyes to his, "If men as clever as you are willing to be among the oppressors of women, what can one expect of ordinary men?"

"You think that I am an oppressor of women?" he said, immensely pleased.

She did not answer.

He looked about him and wondered how much time was left before lunch. He was thinking it was time to turn back. Eleanor, looking up at him and seeing that his attention had wandered away from her although it was their last talk together, could not help letting a reproachful expression appear on her face.

He came close to her and took her arm.

"Why do you disapprove of me so much, Miss Eleanor?"

She looked at him gravely, glad that he was at last prepared to be serious. "I don't disapprove of you, only I have been a little angry since that night."

"Since what night?" he asked, completely mystified.

"Since New Year's night," she said in a much quieter voice than she had expected.

It still did not dawn on Mr Premiss what she meant. She looked up at him, but she blushed and looked down again. It suddenly occurred to him.

""Why! Because I kissed you!" he said in surprise.

She nodded.

"But didn't you like it?" he asked, quite unable for the moment to enter into her feelings.

She was profoundly shocked.

He pressed her arm tightly to make her look up again. "What is wrong, Miss Eleanor?"

"I think you are a flirt," she whispered, and when she had pronounced the awful word she looked up to see its effect, fearful at her own daring, but relieved at having made this stand for truth.

"But you can't object to my being a flirt," he said, dropping her arm and looking up to the sky. He had forgotten for the moment that he was in a hurry.

"But I thought a flirt was a person who tried to break people's hearts!" she said, rather thrown off her argument by his acquiescence.

"Why, Miss Eleanor," he said, "in this world we poor mortals stand alone, rather far from each other, and it is not altogether easy for us to meet. But when one makes love a little – not too much – it is like sending little messengers out to communicate with each other. If you were ever so kind as to condescend to flirt with me, it would be like a little white dove flying towards me," he laughed. "And I should send to you – what bird do you think I should send?"

"A kingfisher," she said spontaneously.

Premiss laughed softly to himself, pleased with what he

considered a compliment. "We must turn back," he said. "I have a lot more to do." He smiled at her, but she was waiting almost breathlessly for him to go on talking. He tried to remember what he had been saying.

"You see after a time the air would be full of all kinds of nice birds," he said, and laughed.

"But do you forget the people you flirt with afterwards?" she asked anxiously.

He smiled. "I shall never forget you," he promised.

She smiled up at him doubtfully.

"And I shall never, never, never forget your blue eyes."

She met his gaze half-smiling. They were coming near the gate. She was happy and satisfied with the talk with him. She felt very glad that they had now learnt to understand each other better, but she said, "Perhaps we shall never meet again."

"Oh, yes we shall," he said, hurrying. He looked back at her and laughed.

"I will always be your friend," she said, feeling as if the moment of parting had actually come now that they were at the gate. But he evidently felt that it was quite the same thing to say good-bye to her in the afternoon with all the others there.

"You will always be my little darling," he said, and left her at the gate and ran into the house to finish his packing.

In the afternoon he went away. The others were all there when he said good-bye, and George was trying to make him hurry to the station, and he was rather distraught because he could not remember if he had put in a book he wanted to read in the train. She would have had no opportunity to talk to him. She stood at the side of the gate and watched him go down the hill. He waved his handkerchief but he did not look back. She felt that she was being faithful to him; Olivia went into the house the minute he was outside the gate. She felt sad, but she could not help thinking of the kingfisher, and she felt that he had given her a lot of ideas.

The next morning she met Mr Nettle on the hill further up

than the house. He looked pale and even thinner. A scarf was wrapped round his thin neck, and the collar of his overcoat was half turned up. It was the first time he had been out since he was ill. He had that air of convalescents of being very careful of his newly recovered energy, and when Eleanor spoke to him, he shook hands with her and smiled without saying anything. She felt that he looked pathetic, and she thought of what Mr Premiss had said about people in this world standing alone, rather far from each other. She smiled at him and said, "We have missed you, you know. It won't be at all nice of you if you get ill again."

Nettle smiled at her once more without speaking.

"Do you still feel ill?" she asked.

"No," he said, "but a little tired sometimes. It is after staying in the house so long."

"Yes, of course, that must make one awfully tired," she said sympathetically. Then she looked at him sideways with a little smile and said, "Why is it that you never will talk to me, Mr Nettle?"

Nettle looked on the ground in embarrassment at being accused this decisively of his particular fault. But when he looked up and saw that she had intended the remark for a sort of joke, although he did not quite understand her, he gave a perplexed smile.

Eleanor stopped rather discouraged, and really did not know what to say next to him. So she walked along at his side, looking at the road and thinking.

"Is Mr Premiss still staying with you?" asked Nettle suddenly on his own account.

"No," she said. "He went yesterday."

"Who was he?" he asked.

"You mean what he is?" she said. "He is a very distinguished critic, quite famous. If you would like, George could lend you one of his books. They are essays. He is a great friend of George's. Did you like him?"

"Yes," said Nettle in a deeply respectful voice, and looked sadly on the ground.

They did not go far but turned together and walked back. She began to talk to him again.

"Now that Mr Premiss is gone I have really no one to talk to me," she said, "so I think you ought to make up your mind to talk to me at least now at this moment."

Nettle looked up at her with such an apprehensive and forlorn look that she was really taken aback, and she looked at his pale face, and instead of continuing the conversation she impulsively invited him to lunch. But he refused to come, because he said that his landlady would have prepared it for him, and that he ought to go home.

"I am so glad you feel better," she said seriously, shaking hands with him at the gate.

He felt that she had been very kind to him and he smiled at her again. Then he went down the hill. He was tired. He could hear some sheep crying in the fields. He went slowly, looking at the ground and thinking. He was quite happy, and felt a pleasure in the need of making the little energy that remained to him after his walk last out until he reached the house. He smiled with pleasure at the thought of Eleanor and how she had talked to him about Mr Premiss, and he realised that she was a very beautiful girl. When he got home he sat down in his chair, even without taking off his coat, for a long time to rest.

The snow came once more, and this time stayed on the ground for a few days until it was trodden underfoot and dirty, and when the sun, shining gloomily through cold grey clouds, had begun to melt it, it still remained clinging to the shaded branches of the fir trees, and on the top of the hill, and in narrow sheltered lanes.

Olivia never liked to go out when it snowed. She looked from her window at the white landscape. It gave her a curious and unpleasant feeling of helplessness to see the earth quite hidden from her sight, as if it were perhaps no longer really beneath her feet. The snow glittered coldly. The grey sky looked coldly down through the white branches of the bare trees. There was no shelter anywhere. Olivia stood looking from the window. She stood quite motionless except that she put her hand up against her cheek to feel how cold it was. Her large, sad eyes looked out on the snow.

But Eleanor went out into the garden and through the gate. She looked round with her blue eyes at the white monotonous countryside. It made her feel like a bird whom no obstacle prevents from spreading its wings and flying to and fro over the earth, now coming in a low, swooping flight to the ground, now wheeling up to the low, grey sky. Here and there the branches of fir trees with their dark bluish-green half hidden by the snow stood silently against the sky. The hedges and the copses of leafless trees were like clouds of shining white mist, or like fine lace, through which the sky seemed a darker grey.

At night the sky was starry. The little stars looked down eagerly with their cold little eyes. But next day there were grey clouds, and the branches of the trees were now bare and grey. The snow, except for a few patches on the fields and on the hill, disappeared, and the earth came to sight again.

When the snow was quite gone, Olivia came out and walked by herself along the grey road. Since Mr Premiss had gone there seemed nothing to do in the house. She walked along looking at the ground, and then she looked at the flat fields and the trees, and at the farmhouse near the road whose dark grey walls only showed here and there through the misty black trees which surrounded it. She looked at it all half without seeing it, and then walked on.

When she got back to the house Eleanor was in the garden near one of the fir trees. She looked up as Olivia came through the gate.

"Oh, Olivia, do come and see," she said. "There are some snowdrops coming up."

Olivia smiled faintly and walked across the grass towards her. She stopped and looked down without bending her head. There, where the thick dark branches of the little fir tree sheltered the garden from the wind, the whitish-green leaves of snowdrops were pushing their blunt tops up through the hard earth.

"Aren't they charming?" said Eleanor. "How long do you think they will take to have flowers?"

"I don't know," said Olivia, looking down wearily at the little leaves.

"There are only these," said Eleanor. "I wish we had thought of planting a lot of them."

Olivia was silent and her dark eyes gazed abstractedly at the trunks of the fir trees and at the light, hard earth of the garden. George came across the grass in a black suit with his hands in his pockets.

"What's the matter?" he asked.

Eleanor lifted her blue eyes to him and smiled. "Only snowdrops," she said. "Come and see."

George walked up to them in a dignified manner, and after a passing glance at the little snowdrops, he began to talk about something else. With his hands in his pockets he looked across the garden down to the road.

Olivia did not listen to what he was saying, nor to Eleanor answering him. A sudden feeling of loneliness had come upon her, so intense, that the place and the people around her, the hard, stony garden and the trees, stood out empty and bare as though without any deeper implications, as though she had withdrawn into herself all the imagination and affection which could have given them life and depth. She felt in that moment an almost intolerable distaste for life, a kind of nausea.

She began half-unconsciously to listen to what they were saying. Eleanor had said something to George and he answered her a little impatiently.

"I can't help it," said Eleanor, "but I think you are talking nonsense."

George looked round with an aggrieved expression. "I don't know how it is. Eleanor never agrees with a word I say nowadays."

Eleanor laughed.

George turned to Olivia for support, but she was turning away and walking slowly towards the house. With another glance at Eleanor of interrogation and reproach, he followed her.

Eleanor looked again at the snowdrop leaves. It was some weeks now since Mr Premiss had gone away. She thought that perhaps he would have sent her a little note. But he had only written to George and sent polite messages to them all. She looked around the garden and sighed. She found in these days very little to do with herself. She was tired of reading. She wandered from room to room looking for someone to talk to, and sometimes she stood for hours and hours at the window looking out.

The wind was now often very strong and cold. It flung the tree branches together until they rattled like bones, until one waited to see the rooks' nests in the high trees come falling down. But they always stayed firm, swaying with the swinging of the branches. Eleanor stood watching the wind rushing across the earth making everything bend before it, blowing down upon the hardened ground as if it wished to penetrate below its cold surface. She found it fascinating to watch its great force, but she was in a way appalled at its terrible, unnecessary fury.

While she stood there watching she saw Pauline Clark coming along the road in her old greenish-grey coat, blown into all sorts of shapes by the wind. Her hands were hidden in the sleeves to keep them warm. She formed so effectively a part of the scene that it did not occur to Eleanor to beckon to her to come to the house, as she looked searchingly up at the windows, though this was what Pauline had come for, not just to walk about in the biting wind.

Eleanor turned away from the window with a yawn. Still yawning she went out into the hall and met George hurrying across from the kitchen with a pencil in his hand. He had a peculiarly serious and worried expression on his face. She looked at him for a minute without thinking of anything to say, though she was so bored that she would have been glad of anything in the nature of a conversation. Then suddenly recollecting it, she told him that she had promised that he should lend Mr Nettle his volume of Mr Premiss's essays.

"Are you going to see him to-night?" she asked.

George shook his head emphatically. "No, I am much too busy," he said.

She went away wondering what on earth he could be so busy with. But soon she got so tired of walking about with nothing to do that she conceived the idea of taking the book down to Mr Nettle herself. She fetched it from George's room, and having at last found something to occupy her, she could not restrain herself from hurrying down the hill at once, although she knew that he did not come from work until six o'clock, and she reached his house before he was home. Mrs Clark took her into his room to wait, and went out to put a clean apron on. Eleanor sat there and waited. She felt a little awkward because, of course, she could have left the book and gone away. Mr Nettle's tea was laid ready for him, and it made her feel as though she had invited herself to tea. The tea was laid quite nicely, only there was a jam-pot on the table. She felt suddenly very sorry for him that he should have to spend his life here alone and without such things as jam dishes.

Mrs Clark came in again.

"He doesn't get home until quarter past six, Miss."

"Doesn't he?" said Eleanor politely, looking at the clock.

She thought that perhaps Mrs Clark wanted to thank her for giving Pauline the beads, and to make it easier for her she said, "How is your daughter?"

Mrs Clark looked at the fire and said in a hard voice, "She'll drive me to my grave."

Eleanor looked at her in surprise and alarm.

"You don't know her, Miss. She's not to be trusted out of sight. She think of nothing but running after the boys. It would serve her right if I turned her out of the house."

"Oh, Mrs Clark," said Eleanor anxiously.

"Well, I can't keep her here much longer," said Mrs Clark, stretching out her long hands. "She can work when she wants to, but when she gets a sulky fit I can't do anything with her. But with a stranger she would be all right, you'd see."

"Then can't you find some work for her somewhere else?" asked Eleanor gravely.

"Where can I get a place for her, Miss?" said Mrs Clark, looking at her intently.

"I don't know," said Eleanor puzzled.

"You don't know whether your aunt wants another maid?" said Mrs Clark, watching her rather slyly.

Eleanor looked up in surprise. "You mean at our house?"

"Yes, Miss," said Mrs Clark eagerly. "I don't want to send her away where I can't keep my eye on her, and it would be a nice training for her to come up with you."

Eleanor looked at her in perplexity. "But would she like it?" she asked.

"You let me hear her say that," said Mrs Clark threateningly. "You ask your aunt, Miss, if she's got a place for her."

"Well, I don't think we can possibly have a place," said Eleanor. "But perhaps we will have some day."

"She can wait. You ask your aunt."

"I'll ask my sister," Eleanor said very doubtfully. "She has quite as much to do with it as my aunt, you know. But don't tell her yet, please, because of course I can't be sure."

Mrs Clark suddenly called to the kitchen. "Bring in another cup and saucer this minute."

Pauline came in. She stood with the cup and saucer in her hand, and looked at Eleanor without smiling and with curiosity. Eleanor smiled at her rather guiltily because they had been talking about her. Her mother took the things out of her hand impatiently and put them on the table. She looked at the clock and said, "It's five and twenty past already. He's late to-day."

Eleanor looked at the clock too.

"He isn't coming," said Pauline suddenly, still looking at her.

"What do you mean by that?" said her mother.

"He's gone to tea and supper with his uncle," said Pauline. "He told me dinner-time."

"Then why didn't you say so before?" asked her mother angrily.

"I forgot," said Pauline, smiling and beginning to walk out of the room.

"Aren't you ashamed of yourself, making me lay tea and keeping the young lady waiting like this?"

"Well, I can't help it if I forgot. Can I?" said Pauline.

"You wait," said Mrs Clark in a low, angry voice.

Pauline shrugged her shoulders and went out through the doorway. But before she was quite out of the room her mother in a fury gave her a violent push and shut the door after her.

Eleanor was very much embarrassed. She would have liked to explain that she had not minded being kept waiting, but the moment for doing so had gone, so she only said that she would not stay any longer and she hurried home. The little scene had rather upset her ideas, and she wondered now how she could possibly have gone there believing that she could have anything approaching a conversation with Mr Nettle. She was in a way sorry that she had missed him, and thought about the matter on the way up the hill, but Pauline and her mother continued to come into her mind and drive away her other thoughts. She had forgotten to leave the book after all, and she was carrying it up the hill again. But after this she gave up the idea of taking it down for him, because she did not like to call again at his house, and she thought it would do when he came up to visit them.

This did not happen at once, for he did not come so far while it was windy. He wrapped a scarf around his neck, and turned up his coat collar to go to and from the post-office. He was feeling much better, but he was afraid of the wind. He had decided to stay on even after winter was over. He had a deep longing to see the summer here in the same place, to feel the ground which had always been hard and cold soften beneath his feet, and to see the bare, skeleton-like trees covered with delicate, green leaves. He almost smelt the air to see if Spring were coming, but up to now there was no suspicion of Spring in the air nor any trace of it on the hard earth. Nettle felt a great deal of new life in himself which only needed something to awaken it, some warmth or the fresh, tender beauty of budding trees.

By this time there were little green buds on Eleanor's snowdrops, and one or two yellow and purple and white crocuses were coming up right in the middle of the grass in the garden.

Eleanor, because she had nothing to do, walked along the roads and through the fields. Usually she did not notice the things around her, but sometimes, now, she stopped and looked at the grey trees or at the tangle of bare, grey twigs in a hedge, and although there was no sign in them yet of Spring, the fact that they were really preparing to burst into life, that all that life was imprisoned in them, made them seem already not so barren and dead. For this reason she picked one without thinking and carried it home, only then realising that it was of no use, she left it lying on the garden path.

Sometimes now the sky was no longer grey but filled with great white clouds, and the wind blew them swiftly across the sky, and it was left blue and almost cloudless, only the wind was still cold and the trees still grey and bare. But the blue sky tempted everyone out. Mrs Curle walked through the village and George went for a walk with Olivia and Eleanor.

They went along for some time in silence, but then Olivia suddenly looked up and said, "The winter seems to have gone so slowly. I was thinking of when Mr Premiss came here. It seems ages since then."

"Why, I think it has gone quickly!" said Eleanor in surprise. "Just think, it is nearly two terms since I left school, not counting the holidays."

"Oh, of course time flies when one is young," said George sententiously. "We are getting old," he smiled affectionately at Olivia, but she did not look up and walked on, looking at the ground.

"Still it *is* funny," said Eleanor, and then because evidently something had suddenly flashed into her head, she stopped talking and was silent for a long time.

George walked along feeling in a very good temper. He had come upon an idea just after breakfast, and he would have liked to expound it, but both the girls were so deeply plunged in thought that he did not want to disturb them, and besides it had occurred to him lately that one should perhaps give things time to mature in one's mind before talking about them. So he, too, was silent.

The sun was shining and the wind, which chased some little white clouds across the sky, blew through the grey branches of the trees. But although the sun shone it was very cold. The trees looked pale grey and bare under the blue sky.

George looked around him suddenly, and with a certain air of positiveness made some remark about the relations of man to nature which *did* perhaps call for criticism.

"Oh, George, what nonsense," said Eleanor quickly.

He looked rather hurt and turned to Olivia. "Do you know," he said, "I have only to open my mouth lately and Eleanor prepares to disagree with what I am going to say."

Olivia smiled at her.

"The world is getting too small for her," she said.

"Oh," said George solemnly, raising his eyebrows. Then he smiled at Eleanor and said, "If she is only a chicken pecking at its shell I forgive her. But it would most certainly create a scandal if the first thing a chicken did when it came into the light of day were to contradict its elders." He suddenly laughed benevolently.

Eleanor laughed, but seeing that he was becoming serious again and evidently preparing to talk, she ran on a little way and walked along by herself. She felt very happy and gay. It seemed to her at that moment that the whole world might have been contained within herself. It made her feel as if everything around her were on the point of springing into life. But under the blue sky the hard, bare fields and the grey branches of the trees resisted half-lifelessly the beating of the wind.

She looked back. George and Olivia were talking gravely. It seemed to her that Olivia looked grave and sad. She turned and went soberly on for a few minutes, but it is as impossible to suppress gaiety as it would be for a bird to try not to sing.

But when they turned to go home, she got tired of walking alone, and she took Olivia's arm and walked at her side. They did not speak, except that George made some remarks that did not require answers. Olivia seemed to have forgotten them both. She was looking at the ground and thinking. Eleanor looked up at her sideways. When she glanced down like that, and her eyes were hidden by their lids and only the black lashes showed on her pale cheeks, she looked very beautiful. Eleanor had always been proud of her ever since she could remember. She squeezed her arm tightly. Olivia looked up. Eleanor laughed. Olivia only smiled a little and looked down again and went on thinking. Eleanor, too, began to be lost in her thoughts.

Mrs Curle, when she was coming through the village to go back to the house, passed Pauline Clark on the road. She frowned at her, but Pauline smiled her rather insolent smile and stopped as if she expected her to speak. But neither the sunshine nor Pauline's smile had a softening effect on Mrs Curle. She nodded her head severely and walked past. Pauline looked after her with a critical glance, and then shrugging her shoulders turned in at the gate. Mrs Curle walked up the hill, going more and more slowly until she reached the house. When she got there she looked through the rooms for the others, or more particularly for her son, and not finding him, came out again with her hat and coat still on and went up the road to meet them in the direction in which they had gone.

Arnold Nettle coming home from work thought that he would like to go up and see them that evening. Only when he thought of the wind and the cold night air he decided to wait for a few days longer. And in the evening he sat indoors. He felt practically well now, but instead of doing anything he sat quietly looking at the fire.

Outside in the moonlight the trees rippled and rustled in the wind. The branches of the fir trees outside Olivia's window seemed to sweep the air around them and were not silent during the whole night. Olivia lay in bed listening to them until she fell into a deep but troubled sleep. The moonlight shone in on the wall to the right of her bed. She was dreaming, and one of her hands sometimes clung tightly to the frill of the pillow, and once or twice her head moved from side to side as if in her sleep she wished to deny something. The reflection of the moon moved slowly across the room, at one time shining on her face, and disappeared. Then morning came.

When Olivia awoke she got out of bed and went to the window in her nightdress to look out. She stood there looking down at the garden and shivered a little from the cold as she slowly brushed her black hair. She felt rather tired, and there hung about her a vague and unexplained sensation of unhappiness. During the morning, while she was busy, it sank into the background, so that it seemed no longer to be there, but just before lunch as she walked down to the village it came to the surface again. She had promised Eleanor that she would call to see Mrs Clark and discuss Pauline with her. At the house she met Pauline herself coming out. Pauline smiled and walked on, and Olivia went in.

When she was coming out again Mr Nettle met her. He was coming from his work. He smiled shyly and stood in front of her before the doorstep waiting for her to speak. She looked at him for a moment without smiling, trying to recall her thoughts. He stood there with his head held a little awkwardly on one side and neither moved nor said anything, but smiled with such a naïve trust in her kindness that her conscience suddenly smote her for not being more pleased to see him after he had been ill.

She smiled at him with serious eyes.

"I have not seen you since just after Christmas," she said. "Are you quite better?"

He nodded and smiled with more certainty.

"You looked very ill then," she said. She paused and looked at him. "You are quite better now?"

"Yes," he said, not taking his eyes off her, as if he had something important that he was waiting for an opportunity to say.

She looked up the road.

"We have been expecting to see you," she said, looking round at him again.

"The wind is too cold in the evenings," he explained.

She did not answer, but smiled and began to walk away.

He put out his hand shyly. They shook hands and she went up the road towards the hill. He stood watching her and then he went into the house.

In the afternoon she went and lay down on her bed. She read for a short time, but then she let her book fall and lay, looking lazily through the window at the sky. Eleanor came to find her, and tapped at the door.

"May I come in?" she asked.

"Yes," said Olivia without moving her head.

Eleanor stood and looked down at her.

"I won't talk to you if you are trying to sleep," she said.

Olivia smiled, and Eleanor, thinking that this implied doubt of her ability to keep silent, laughed as she went to the window. She sat down, half-kneeling on the window seat, and looked down at the garden and the tops of the fir trees. She sat there quite silent, thinking, only once she turned to Olivia with her lips tightly pressed together to show that she was not talking. Olivia was amused and she smiled, but Eleanor had already turned back to her contemplation of the garden, and Olivia, too, returned to her own thoughts.

Outside, the wind rustled the green branches of the firs. The bare branches of the grey, leafless trees moved in the wind with so regular a motion that the whole tree seemed to be swaying from side to side as if giddy and intoxicated by the sight of the blue sky. The sun shone on the roads and on the pavements in the village.

Pauline Clark came out on to the door-step of her house and stood there looking up and down the road. Nobody was in sight in either direction. She turned her head and called into the house: "I'm going out."

Her mother did not answer, but only muttered something. Pauline, paying no attention, fetched her coat and looked up and down again trying to decide in which direction to go. She went up walking half on the pavement and half on the side of the road. But she did not meet anyone in this direction so she turned and went back, past her own house and through the village.

Mr Nettle saw her passing the post-office. He sat upright at his table to watch the short, thick-set figure go slowly along the road. He wondered for a moment where she was going to in such a leisurely manner. But after that she went out of his mind. He felt that day particularly energetic, so that he was even restless and looked nervously from side to side, and continually scraped his chair along the floor until it was time to go home. He put his shoulders back and walked briskly along the road. Even now he was not tired. He thought again of going to Olivia's house, although the wind blew as strongly as ever, but then he had the idea of practising that evening on his cello, which he had not touched since he was ill.

Immediately after tea he took it out of its case and began to play. But half-way through the evening George Curle came to see him. He sat down in the armchair and then looked up with a slightly despondent air at Nettle who, as stealthily as possible, so that his movements should not disturb his visitor's thoughts, was putting the cello back into its case. George rested his head on his hand and waited until Nettle was ready to sit down. He began then to explain why he had not called before. He began to say that he had been very busy, but either because the statement seemed to need modification or because he had forgotten where he was, and what he was saying, he broke off this remark in the middle and began to look at the fire.

Nettle sat upright in his chair and observed him with unobtrusive curiosity, and when George looked up he was a little confused because of this, and hurriedly changed his expression. George began to talk again, but scarcely with his usual flow of good spirits. It appeared that he had been in a very despondent mood about his work. Nettle would have liked to reassure him in some manner, but he could find no way of expressing his feelings about George's immense learning and cleverness. He listened with a kind of alarmed air, and he felt for the time a little damped.

George did not stay very long, and seemed not to have noticed that Nettle had scarcely said a word all the time that he was there. He walked up the hill to the house, still feeling rather subdued. The moon was shining. He dug his hands into his coat pockets and began to whistle monotonously under his breath. This did not in any way raise his spirits. He had not at all his usual feeling of self-confidence. Above his head the black, topmost branches of the trees swayed back and fore against the pale, misty, moonlit sky. The moon shone right on to the house. The black tops of the fir trees moved stiffly from side to side. George sighed a little as he went along the path to the house. He opened the door with his key and went in. Eleanor was in the hall just going upstairs. She stopped at the bottom and turned to look at him, smiling half-questioningly.

"Where are you going?" he asked.

"Bed," she said, "but everyone is going in a minute."

She went upstairs, and George stood watching her. She smiled half-coquettishly over her shoulder because she thought he was looking up at her and laughing, but he had in fact a puzzled and worried expression on his face. He went in to talk to the others. Olivia was already standing up and she went away almost at once. He sat and talked to his mother and then went to bed. But he could not sleep for a long time. He lay not unpleasantly, looking at the soft grey sky, and stopped thinking about himself and his troubles and desires.

Nettle, too, could not sleep. After the temporary depression that George's serious mood had given to his good spirits, the pleasant sensation of energy that he had had in the afternoon came back to him, and made him think of things vividly and excitably. It was that morning that he had seen

Olivia again. And even in the middle of thinking of their meeting he thought of George's self-critical remarks, and it impressed him very much to realise how these people who seemed to him not to possess any of the customary human failings should be so full of humility.

He was a little tired the next day, but as he walked quietly to and from the post-office, everything that he saw and noticed seemed to him interesting enough to remember and perhaps to talk about when he went once more to see his friends. It was curious that he felt no impatience for the visit, but even a kind of pleasure in putting it off from day to day.

Eleanor came into the post-office to buy stamps, and as she stood at the counter she smiled gaily across to his table. He looked up at her and then smiled shyly. She glanced back again and nodded as she went out. She felt very gay and could scarcely stop herself from singing as she went up the hill in the sunshine. There was only a little blue sky left. At one side of the sky, grey clouds were piled up and the wind blew them slowly along and swung the grey branches of the trees, and tumbled Eleanor's hair. She would have stayed in the garden, but it was too cold standing still. She went once slowly along the garden beds to see if anything besides the snowdrops was coming up. After that she went into the house. She flung her coat down on a chair and went to look for Olivia. In the drawing-room she found Mrs Curle sitting in the middle of the room knitting.

"Where's Olivia?" Eleanor asked.

Mrs Curle did not answer but looked up rather petulantly.

"Do you know where Olivia is, Auntie?" asked Eleanor again.

"You must do your hair," said Mrs Curle sulkily and as if she had already said this once or twice.

"Oh, Auntie," said Eleanor, throwing it over her shoulder and frowning. "I've only just come in. It's the wind."

Mrs Curle did not answer. Eleanor looked down at her

rather angrily, but seeing that she was not going to say anything more she shook her head and looked up at the ceiling wondering what to do next.

"You are an idle girl," said her aunt suddenly.

"Idle!" she repeated in surprise.

"When I was young girls did not sit about all day doing nothing."

"But Auntie, I don't do nothing. I read a lot."

"We used to do our sewing," Mrs Curle went on, looking straight in front of her in an accusing manner.

"Yes, things that were no use to anybody after all," Eleanor said, and she went to the window and stood looking out on to the garden.

"It's not right to be so idle," Mrs Curle began again.

Eleanor turned to answer with a gesture of impatience, but at that moment George came in, so instead of saying anything she stopped short. Mrs Curle went on perseveringly.

"It is my duty to correct you. You mustn't waste your time."

"What's the matter?" asked George, coming forward into the room and looking seriously from one to the other.

"She says I'm lazy," said Eleanor, looking up at him and finding it very difficult not to laugh.

"Oh," said George reproachfully, though Eleanor could not at first tell to whom the reproach was addressed.

Mrs Curle went on looking in front of her with a stupid and obstinate expression on her face.

"What has she done?" said George anxiously.

"She does nothing," said Mrs Curle.

"Oh," said George in protest.

"She is an idle girl," said his mother.

George, looking up, caught Eleanor's smile. He smiled rather unwillingly himself, and growing hurriedly serious said, " But I think it is right for young people to be idle."

Mrs Curle did not answer. Eleanor looked at him in surprise.

"You know," he said, putting his head to rest on his hand and looking up at the ceiling with a rather innocent expression on his face, "when one is young one is able to live unconsciously and contentedly in a kind of idleness that presupposes the vanity of all human aspirations. Now is not that, by some paradox, the very thing that one afterwards takes years of considerable anguish to learn? Can it then be advisable to eliminate it as a phase of growth?"

Eleanor was much struck with his.

His mother shrugged her shoulders heavily.

"Nonsense," she remarked.

"It is not nonsense," he said gently, with forbearance.

"When I was young girls used to sew," said his mother.

George smiled. "Can't you sew?" he asked Eleanor.

"Of course, if I try," she said.

He smiled benevolently at them both, then becoming at once serious he began to talk in rather abstract terms but still, it seemed, in Eleanor's defence. She, however, found it hard to keep her attention on what he said, and began to think of something else, until George, pausing to emphasise something, caught an inattentive look in her eye. She smiled at him as though she were innocent of deserving any reproach of ingratitude and tried to listen more carefully. But when George had ceased to regard her suspiciously she began to look out of the window from where she was standing, at the sky, which was gradually becoming covered with grey clouds. Since Mrs Curle did not take George's remarks in the deeply philosophical spirit they were meant, and by and by brought the conversation down to a very personal level, on which George did not show up so well, it soon ceased to have any application to Eleanor. So she went right up to the window, leaned against the frame, and looked out. She turned round once, surprised at the vexation with which George was meeting a rather foolish accusation from his mother. She sighed a little to herself.

She stayed at the window even after the others had gone out of the room. Soon afterwards George appeared in the garden walking to and fro on the grass so quickly and evidently in rather a bad temper, that once he seemed on the point of treading on one of the little crocuses in the middle of the grass. Eleanor stood still in anxiety, for it seemed too late even to knock on the window and warn him. But he saw it before he put his foot down and, carefully walking over it, he continued his perambulations to and fro.

By now the sky had quite clouded over and not a patch of blue was left. The wind dropped, and in the afternoon a thin, warm rain began to fall. Olivia was in the village when it came. The rain was so fine as to be little more than a mist. She walked slowly up the hill feeling it pleasantly on her face. She stood in the garden looking at it covering the valley with a grey cloud. The hard earth of the garden and the fir trees absorbed the rain quickly and yet scarcely seemed to be moistened themselves. Olivia stood there thinking and not heeding the rain for a few minutes before she entered the house.

In the evening, while Eleanor stood at the window watching the sky growing darker, Olivia sat and looked at her and at the rainy garden beyond her. Sometimes Eleanor turned round to say something, but Olivia answered her only by smiling. Even when it was quite dark outside and Eleanor came from the window and sat down to read, Olivia sat as before, thinking.

When she went to bed she lay there without sleeping and listened to the faint rustling of the fine rain upon the little fir trees and looked with open eyes at the black, starless sky, until her thoughts gradually faded into sleep.

The next day the sky was a dull white. The grey bare trees and the pale green fields scarcely showed that the rain had refreshed them. After the wind the still, immovable branches of the trees and the unchanging, dull white of the sky gave to everything an air of permanence, motionlessness, and even silence. The fir trees seemed to keep an untiring vigil over the hard earth of the garden beds. There was upon everything the breathless silence which a day of bright sunshine sometimes gives to a landscape of fields, only this was something more subdued and impregnated with a monotonous melancholy. The day itself seemed to stand still, moving imperceptibly towards its unemphatic yielding to night, which came down upon it like a deep heavy shadow and next morning vanished again.

Eleanor went out to pick the snowdrops from the garden and take them into the house. And that evening Mr Nettle decided to go up there again. He came home from the post-office feeling a kind of excitement at the thought of visiting them, but much more than at that he was excited at feeling well. And it was pleasant walking through the warm, damp air when there was no wind.

After tea he rested for a while by the fire. Then he set out. As he came out of the door Pauline Clark had just crossed the road on her way to choir practice. She stood at the churchyard gate and looked round at him. He smiled shyly at her. She laughed and kept looking at him, probably remarking where he was going. He heard someone call her from the church porch and when he looked round again she had disappeared.

He walked slowly up the hill. It was just beginning to get dark. The greyness of the day had turned into a darker, less transparent greyness. The sharp outlines of the trees had grown softer, and the shadows wrapped around them gave to the whole scene a gentler and calmer air. The twilight deepened as Nettle ascended the hill. The atmosphere was like a low-pitched monotonous phrase in some music, only Nettle was in such an excitable mood and had a feeling of such extraordinary happiness that he might have been singing an octave above it, a long, sustained song of joy. And he felt like that all the way there, but when he reached the gate of the house his old feeling of nervousness attacked him. He stood for a moment looking at the windows with wide-open, timid eyes. His hand groped for the latch of the gate, but it was on the wrong side. He had to look down to find it. He shut it very quietly so that they should not hear from the house. Then he walked slowly along the path. He had to stand for a minute outside the door before knocking. His heart was beating quickly with the climb and because he had not been there since he was ill. Then he knocked.

George, coming to open the door put his head on one side and smiled at him with satisfaction, and was really very pleased to see him there again. He stopped in the doorway of the drawing-room to say, "Do you know who is here?"

Only Eleanor was sitting where she could see Nettle standing behind George's back. She looked up at him with a smile of welcome. He smiled timidly and uncertainly back. George led him into the room. Olivia was there. She was pleased to see him too. She smiled at him kindly. Mrs Curle pointed to a seat next to hers and he sat down in it. He felt happy at being there once more and he sat smiling at them all, forgetting the necessity of speaking.

He still looked rather ill, they thought, at any rate worse than when he first came there. He was tired now with his walk up the hall. He sat there and smiled at them, but he did not talk now any more than before. Eleanor looked at him and suddenly felt rather sorry for him and wondered why for him there should be so many difficulties about life, as it seemed to her at that moment that there were.

On the table the little snowdrops that she had picked stood in all their green and white innocence like children, singing with thin, childish voices a sort of New Year's hymn. Nettle was very fond of flowers. He looked at them and smiled with pleasure, quite unconscious that the others were noticing him. He felt rested and at peace with everything. He forgot that he ought to talk.

"Are you quite well?" asked Mrs Curle.

"Yes," he said, scarcely conscious of what the question meant.

Olivia smiled at him with her dark eyes. He sat still, looking at her. He suddenly remembered something. He turned and leaned towards Mrs Curle and said, "Thank you very much for what you sent me when I was ill."

She nodded tolerantly. He felt very glad that he had not forgotten.

"Oh," said Eleanor, standing up suddenly, "I'll get the book for you so that you won't forget it."

Nettle looked up questioningly. Olivia was smiling at him and he was a little confused. Eleanor came back with Mr Premiss's book and put it on the table by his side for him to take it home.

"You must tell us what you think of it," she said kindly, though she did not really think that he would be able to give an opinion on it.

He would have liked to look inside the book, but he thought that it would be impolite to show his curiosity before them. He smoothed the cover gently with his hand.

Outside the window it was already quite dark. There was scarcely any wind and only the fir trees rustled faintly in the garden. The sharply outlined naked trees were hidden in the soft folds of the night, which gave to the barren earth an appearance of fertility and fruitfulness, only it was a fertility with no gifts for mankind. There was a new moon. The little fir trees threw a faint shadow on to the path.

In the room, almost unconscious of where he was, Nettle sat and looked at Olivia. And he could do so quite naturally tonight because she was in a particularly vivacious and even gay mood and talked much more than usual.

When George was speaking she looked down, her eyelids lowered over her large eyes, her eyelashes overshadowing her pale cheeks and her hands then lay poised like birds resting after a little flight. But when she lifted her head to answer something that he had said her eyelids lifted and her eyes like dark jewels shone out into the room, and her hands fluttered about restlessly on her lap. Her dark hair lay on her head like something sleeping, but breathing a deep and mysterious life. Nettle followed each strand of the plaits with his eyes. Once even she saw his intent and serious gaze, but he met her eyes only for a second and went gravely back to his occupation. Then he studied her face again, watching the shadows that her movements cast on its paleness. It had the immobility, not of a face carved from stone, but one moulded from pale, soft clay.

Suddenly Nettle became aware that they were all looking at him, and he remembered having heard someone speak to him, but he could not recollect whose voice it had been. He looked down in confusion because he did not know whom to answer.

"I believe you were asleep," said Eleanor, laughing up at him. He looked at her and smiled shyly. Everyone laughed, and in spite of his confusion he felt happy again.

At supper he was very careful to listen to the conversation and not to get lost in his own thoughts. But even then he listened, and even took part in it, almost as though he were dreaming it all. They sat around the table like stars, and when they spoke their voices seemed to come to him from far away, as though by some chance the heavens had opened for a minute and a fragment of some angelic conversation had floated down to him upon the earth. With innocent and lonely awe he listened to every word that came from their lips. Olivia's soft, gentle voice was saying half-gaily:

"I wish I could think of something new to pass the time away."

"There are only two ways vouchsafed to us on this plane of existence," said George, smiling with dignity. "You may discourse of philosophy, and you may fall in love."

Eleanor's face lit up with a smile of gaiety and audacity. "Do let us fall in love," she said in her high, clear voice.

Olivia's grew softer, and almost melted into a gentle laugher as it said, "Discoursing of philosophy has less tragic possibilities. That is why George chooses it. Isn't that true, George?"

"Oh come!" said George. "Faust nearly lost his soul; you would only lose your heart."

Olivia considered the matter smiling. "I see that I must be contented with this dull but beatific life," she said.

"Better to be bored in heaven than to make a fuss in hell," said George with a broad smile.

Eleanor gave a ringing laugh.

George was pleased with her appreciation of his little epigram, and, hoping for still more applause, he turned to Nettle and said, "Isn't it?"

They all looked at Nettle. But he, just as if he had really been gazing up at the sky and those ecstatic beings had suddenly looked down on him, continued to gaze at them intently as though his humility did not let him see that it was on him they had turned their angelic glances.

George looked a little disappointed. "Don't you agree with me?" he asked.

Nettle awakened himself. "Yes," he said shyly.

Mrs Curle was talking to the cat and, not noticing that they had become silent, she went on expostulating with it in a mildly severe voice. They listened to her, amused, until Eleanor burst out laughing. Mrs Curle looked round with a mixture of astonishment and indignation, but then she suddenly smiled. They all laughed, and Nettle, too, laughed rather timidly.

Olivia asked him afterwards how much longer he was staying there, for she remembered that he had come only for the winter.

"I am going to stay here always," he admitted.

"You'll get tired of it," said Mrs Curle in her dull voice.

Nettle smiled doubtfully. He would have liked to contradict her and to give his reasons for staying. He tried to think how to put them into words, but he did not think he could describe what he meant. He saw that George was looking at him and smiling with affectionate benevolence. He smiled back at him, and when he went back to his thoughts he found that he had forgotten what he was thinking of before.

He did not stay there very long after supper. He would have liked to stay, but he felt very tired and he had to warn himself to go. He stood up. For a moment they did not realise that he wanted to go since it was still early. He explained. George took him into the hall and, leaving him to put his coat on, opened the door. In a moment, however, Eleanor came running out after them, with Mr Premiss's book in her hand.

"You forgot it," she said rather reproachfully.

"There is a new moon," said George from the doorstep, looking in to see if Nettle was ready.

"Oh, let's go in and look at it," said Eleanor, going to the window and beginning, without looking up at the sky, to open it. Nettle went after her to see if he could help her.

"It's unlucky to look at the new moon through glass," she said.

Nettle, who did not know the superstition, looked from it to her.

"Do you prefer to leave by the window or the door?" she asked smiling, as George came up to them.

Nettle, taking the suggestion seriously, obediently climbed over the window-sill, and stood on the grass waiting to say good-bye.

George laughed. Nettle stood there under the stars smiling shyly back, not quite comprehending. George waved his hand.

"Good-night," he said.

"Good-night," said Nettle.

"Oh, Mr Nettle," said Eleanor, leaning out and calling after him anxiously, "will you be careful not to tread on the crocuses. Some have grown up right in the middle of the grass?"

He looked round to make sure that he had heard what she said, then he went across the garden to the gate, bending his head to look carefully on the ground for the little flowers.

MORE GREAT CLASSICS FROM HONNO

Honno's classics form a unique series which brings books by women writers from Wales, long since out of print, to a new generation of readers.

The Small Mine
Strike for a Kingdom
Travels with a Duchess
You're Welcome to Ulster
Menna Gallie

Four great novels, with introductions by Angela V. John, Claire Connolly and Jane Aaron, one of which, Strike for a Kingdom, was shortlisted for a CWA Gold Dagger Award. Two novels set in mining communities of the Welsh Valleys, one in Yugoslavia in the swinging sixties and one in Northern Ireland at the eve of the Troubles.

Dew on the Grass
The Captain's Wife
Eiluned Lewis

With introductions by
Katie Gramich

An enchanting autobiographical novel of childhood and a lost way of life and a nostalgic look back at a period when the traditional rhythms of traditional Welsh culture were still intact.

Queen of the Rushes:
A Tale of the Welsh Revival
Allen Raine

With introductions by
Katie Gramich

Set at the time of the 1904 Revival, this is an enthralling tale of complex lives and loves that will capture the heart of any modern reader.

A Burglary –
or 'Unconscious Influence'
Amy Dillwyn

With introductions by
Alison Favre

From the author of The Rebecca Rioter, who published six entertaining novels. Clever, yet comic and riveting, this Victorian novel of manners was first published in 1883 in three volumes – known as a 'three-decker'.

ABOUT HONNO

Honno Welsh Women's Press was set up in 1986 by a group of women who felt strongly that women in Wales needed wider opportunities to see their writing in print and to become involved in the publishing process. Our aim is to develop the writing talents of women in Wales, give them new and exciting opportunities to see their work published and often to give them their first 'break' as a writer.

Honno is registered as a community co-operative. Any profit that Honno makes is invested in the publishing programme. Women from Wales and around the world have expressed their support for Honno. Each supporter has a vote at the Annual General Meeting.

To receive further information about forthcoming publications, or become a supporter, please write to Honno at the address below, or visit our website:

www.honno.co.uk

Honno
Unit 14, Creative Units
Aberystwyth Arts Centre
Penglais Campus
Aberystwyth
Ceredigion
SY23 3GL

All Honno titles can be ordered online at
www.honno.co.uk
or by sending a cheque to Honno.
Free p&p to all UK addresses.